On Foreign Ground

a novel by
Eduardo Quiroga

W · W · NORTON & COMPANY
New York   London

Behind me, unclaimed and barren, my youth lies
like dead bones on foreign ground.

Alejandra Pizarnik

Copyright © 1986 by P. A. Brewer
First American Edition 1987

Printed in the United States of America.

Library of Congress Cataloging-in-Publication Data

Quiroga, Eduardo.
   On foreign ground.

   I. Title.
PR9300.9.Q5805   1987   823   86–31084

ISBN 0-393-02448-2

W. W. Norton & Company, Inc., 500 Fifth Avenue, New York, N.Y. 10110
W. W. Norton & Company, Ltd., 37 Great Russell Street, London WC1B 3NU

1 2 3 4 5 6 7 8 9 0

On Foreign Ground

Monday, 10 May 1982

I can see you now, the sun shining softly through the thick red curtains, a smell of lavender coming in through the slightly open window from that lavender bush you told me was just outside your room; I can see you blinking in the new light and stretching and looking at the alarm clock which hasn't worked since you threw it against the wall one winter morning before exams. I see you pushing off the duvet (is it flowered?) and sitting up with a sulk as you always do when you first wake, frowning, letting your hair fall over your eyes. I see you get out (always on the right side; remember the fuss you made that time because our bed, next to the wall, had only a left side to it?) and walk barefoot to the bathroom. You hate slippers. (I liked your warm smell in the mornings, when I could curl up inside your arms or you would put your head, eyes still closed, on my shoulder. I loved your warmth through your nightdress, down your back, between your thighs.) Before you enter the bathroom you pick up the mail the postman just dropped – letters for the other girls? bills? – and then you see my writing. Or maybe you recognize the stamps, the small white Argentine stamps you used to laugh about. Now you are fully awake, you enter the bathroom and close the door, you undress, you run the bath. You won't open the letter until you are lying there, in the hot sweet-smelling bubbles (the one luxury, you used to say, you could not do without) and in the steam you rip open the envelope (carelessly as usual, the way you squeeze the toothpaste in the middle, the way you throw your clothes about when you come in), you tear it open and pull out my letter. This letter, my love, I know you will never read.

1

I long for a hot bath. The grime has stuck to my face like wax and my hair is stiff with dirt. I can almost imagine the smell of toast and coffee and maybe even bacon coming in from the kitchen where Hannah (is that the fat girl's name?) is getting breakfast. I last drank coffee in Buenos Aires; here we get a greenish herb tea, *maté cocido*, a watered-down version of that drink you tried and almost spat out at José's house. Remember? I have been thinking so much of you I feel I can't tell any more what really happened and what I now imagine or dream of. How does your Eliot put it? 'Mixing memory and desire'.

The rain has never stopped since we got here. It's not a fully-fledged rain, it's not a loud, hard rain you can bear with, it doesn't pelt down like angry hammers. This is barely a drizzle: an icy constant curtain, ever-falling, everywhere, like a soft fog, always there, drenching you with a sickening touch, cold, so cold. And the wind. You can hear it beyond the tents; you can hear it whistling behind the hills where the sea is, the black sea around us. You English are accustomed to the sea, it's always with you, a part of your landscape. Your poets are always talking about the sea. Matthew Arnold, you know: 'Now I only hear its melancholy, long, withdrawing roar, retreating to the breath of the night-wind.' But to us it's something foreign. If we come from the provinces, our landscape is the mountains or the plains; if we come from Buenos Aires it's the river – that wide, brown, still river that stretches down to the horizon. Here the sea, like everything that seems to be happening, is alien. It belongs to the world of nightmares. It isn't ours.

Later

Night has fallen but we hardly notice the difference. We lie waiting in our tents; soon we will be marched – we think – towards the battle line. The sergeant tells us that now that the *Sheffield* has been torpedoed, the British will never be able to get into Port Stanley, but won't they? My hand is cramped as I write, the sleeping bag is soaked through; they haven't provided a floor to the tent and the water runs on the plastic sheet from one wall to the other, forming pools in the middle. The soldier next to me is from the North and cannot get accustomed to the cold. We have been told not to touch the roof of the tent because if we do it will leak, but it's almost impossible not to do so. The soldier from the North is big – his name is Samuel – and bangs his head against the roof every time he moves. A drip like Chinese torture falls on him at regular intervals. Now he lies with his eyes wide open, teeth chattering, his copper skin almost grey, staring into the air. He said that in his village they were proud of him and his brother when they left to go down South, 'even further than the Big City'. For him this is another planet, not his country, not even the world as he knows it. For twenty years he had seen nothing but hot parched red land with little white huts and cotton-trees called *algarrobos*; the sun on everything, dry like the cattle bones that line the tracks of his poor province. There were winters of course, but they were different. Sometimes he hums one of the tunes from up there, but most of the time he is silent, while the noise of the incessant drops times the drone of the planes overhead and the bombs which go off somewhere in the growing dark, through the whistling wind, under the rain. Around Samuel's neck hangs a medal with the image of the Chief Namuncurá, Argentina's only Indian saint – unofficial saint, of course – a little Indian chief who betrayed his brothers to the Catholic invaders. Samuel's eyes are a little slanted, like those of Namuncurá.

Tuesday, 11 May 1982

I put myself to sleep thinking of you. I picture you in my mind, throughout the day. Remember when I first saw you? You were leaning against the fountain of the Place Saint-Michel, water gushing down the grey concrete stones above

3

which the young iron archangel is driving his trident into the Devil at his feet. I had left the bunch of tourists I was with – they were heading off to a night of classic Parisian night-life at the Folies Bergères: star-studded plumed dancers for soft-core travellers – and I wanted to be on my own that Christmas Eve. The snow had stopped and the night air was crisp and cold and I followed my breath down the Quai d'Orsay and up the Boulevard Saint-Germain with its bald trees and yellow lights. African souvenir vendors were huddled under blankets on the corners, and by the Café des Deux Magots fire-eaters and jugglers entertained red-nosed customers sitting behind fogged-up café windows sipping their hot sweet wine. Groups of people everywhere were hurrying off to Christmas dinners, whole families with glittering parcels, old gentlemen and fur-clad ladies, boys with funny make-up and girls with gypsy dresses wrapped up in lamb-skin coats or South American ponchos. Cars raced down the boulevard making dirty streaks in the snow, and the green and white buses snorted through the one-way-only corridors, hardly caring for the blinking traffic lights. Towards the Boulevard Saint-Michel – as usual – the crowd grew thicker, bustling by shop windows bright with season's greetings, and there I turned left and walked towards the river. By the time I reached the fountain I was hungry and stopped to buy a cornet of French fries. I took it and sat on the fountain rim watching the cracked ice inside. You stood there – why in the world were you reading out there in the freezing cold? – and as I ate I peered over your shoulder, and read (I remember the lines even now): *Life was a fly that faded, and death a drone that stung; The world was very old indeed when you and I were young.* You turned round and looked at me and I couldn't think what to do, so I offered you a French fry. You laughed and took it and I think I told you then that I had read the book, Chesterton's *The Man Who Was Thursday*, and liked it. 'Good reading for Christmas Eve,' I said. I think you noticed my accent almost immediately (so much for Scottish teachers in Argentine schools) and asked me where I was from, and amazingly you didn't think Buenos Aires was in Brazil. I couldn't stop looking at your eyes, so big and blue in the yellow light overhead. You were wearing a long pink coat and some kind of knitted hat. I told you I was on this coach tour around Europe my parents had given me for my birthday, and that we were staying in Paris two more days. I really felt cold then and asked you if you'd like to have a coffee and you tucked the book away in your pocket and said yes, and as we walked away you said, did I know that the old man at Shakespeare and Co. was offering coffee and doughnuts as a Christmas treat. I knew nothing about Shakespeare and Co. but said yes, let's go there, and as we waited on the kerb for the lights to change you told me about the crazy shop opposite Notre Dame filled with English books and run by an American. It had belonged to a woman, Sylvia Beach, when it stood some twenty blocks away, in the Odéon, and Joyce and Hemingway and Scott Fitzgerald had all used it as general headquarters. Now their ghosts – you said – haunted it, among boxes of second-hand paperbacks and tables of Californian magazines. We pushed open the green door with ad cards stuck to the glass and looked around the room. Wobbly shelves of books towered to the ceiling. A little staircase led to the old man's room upstairs and to a reading room for whoever cared to use it. 'Travellers in reduced circumstances', as the owner called them, were always welcome. George – I think that was the old man's name – was busy heaping doughnuts onto chipped rose-china plates and a girl in a large flowery dress and with plaited hair was doling out cups of black coffee. Quite a number of young people were there, a few looking at the books, most of them just chatting or listening to the music – Pink Floyd or something – that blared out from a tape-recorder. A paper Santa was hanging from the beams on the ceiling and balloons and paper streamers were pinned to the wooden columns. We took our coats off, you took off your hat, shaking your blond hair, and got our coffee and doughnuts.

I must stop now. I can hear the sergeant's voice barking at

5

someone outside. Samuel props himself up on his elbows, looking around as if he doesn't know where he is. I expect we're off on another 'drill'.

Wednesday, 12 May 1982

We're back; it's three in the morning. For a while the sky was full of trailing lights leaving a very slow stream of green behind them. Red fires cross the horizon in flocks of five or six. And the noise of the guns is always there. The hill in front of us is called Two Sisters but our sergeant says we'll change the name and call it after our battalion. During the day it's like a kind of low granite table, rising from the pale green field which slopes down to Port Stanley. I've been there once but the kelpers, the Falklanders, hate us. I feel like a Martian walking across conquered Earth in an old science-fiction movie. The children make faces at us, but the adults seem frightened or angry. Except for a few: the owner of the pub, for instance, gives a fat smile every time he sees one of us come in. He says that he welcomes our poor devalued peso, because he can't use Falkland pounds for anything beyond these rocks. Others are also angry against the British. They don't want *us*, that's for certain, but they don't like the way the British have been treating them either. Third-class citizens, that's what they are, they say. The governor, now safe and snug in England, is made fun of by everyone. He surrendered immediately, it seems, with his seventy-nine soldiers. They call him Paddington because he seems to have come from darkest Peru and needs someone to look after him. But we are despised; we feel, behind these people's eyes, a kind of rage. And the question we can't really answer: Why? Why are we here? We are told that these islands are ours, it has been drummed into our heads ever since playschool. But do we really care? Do *we* really care?

The cold is making my nose run and my hands feel like ice even in the woollen gloves. They tell us that in Buenos Aires, the women gather around the Obelisk and knit gloves like these for us. It is rumoured that these gloves are sold somewhere for some little general's profit. We never know if what they say is true.

I remember the cold that first night in Paris. We walked out of Shakespeare & Co. and down past the Hotel Esmeralda (was that the name of the hunchback's gypsy girl or of her goat?) and on to the church of St Julien, the hunter who shared his bed with a leper. An icy wind with bits of snow began to blow down the Rue St Jacques as we climbed it and it was too cold to talk but it didn't matter, I was feeling so happy. As we got to Jussieu the bells started to peal; we could hear them all the way, from Notre Dame, from St Severin, from St Julien, from the Greek Orthodox Church and from St Michel, and you said you had some spicy tea and we would drink a toast to Christmas. We entered the Rue des Boulangers (you said there was only one baker on that street and terrible at that); we pushed the heavy door into the courtyard and you led the way up the stairs, taking your coat off on the way up, pulling your hat off.

Your flat was tiny; two large windows looking out onto a tree you said had blue flowers in spring, a small kitchen tucked away in a cupboard, a camp bed, a table, two fold-away chairs and a fat persian cat called Gormenghast. You made the scented tea and the smell of spices filled the room and you said it smelt of hot mince pies and mulled wine which I had never tasted. I told you then, I think, about the way we spent our Christmas in the heat of our December summer. I told you about my mother, how she enjoyed cooking that one meal when Cook had her day off, and Father, always anxious about the presents he had bought and carefully hidden, and Juan, my brother, now God knows where, and Ana, my sister, suddenly grown and settled in Brazil. And Granny, of course, who always seemed so small, full of fun, so clever, knowing exactly what everything was about, calling me into her room in the evenings to ask the questions I didn't want asked; Granny baking her special meals for Christmas, Granny just a few years ago, lying even smaller, crumpled like a dry leaf in the bed that looked enormous, saying to us not to mind, she really didn't mind, it had been a long, long road and she had enjoyed every minute of it.

I told you about the house: it was a fine two-storey house with a small front garden, right in the middle of Olivos, in the suburb of Buenos Aires where the English families live. Next door lived the O'Farrells who had met Garibaldi in Buenos Aires, and down the road Mrs Fagin, who had a small lending library of English books, and just behind us, across the road, the seven Nicholson children who were our friends. Our living-room was full of Mother's family portraits, including a miniature said to be of Saint Theresa, from whom Mother said we descended. My mother's grandparents and great-grandparents were all born in Buenos Aires, but before that they came from a small town near Avila, and their dark eyes and slim figures loomed at us from their portraits while we sat around the fire, Mother telling us their stories of unheroic, gentlemanly deeds. Grandmother never cared about that past, but to Mother they were stern reminders of 'the way in which things should be done', and every time we misbehaved she would lift her eyes towards heaven, where she was certain they could hear her, and invoke their many names asking for patience with such wicked children. My father would frown at us, more for upsetting her than for having done something naughty, but the mood of reproval would soon blow over, and the conversation would switch to the latest feat of Rex, our shepherd dog, or to our plans for the holidays.

Monkey, the brother of Ana's boyfriend, would come around on weekends and we'd play complicated games. Monkey had big eyes, red hair and a pug nose, and ears that stood up and always gave him a happy look. One of his favourite games was The English Invasions (the English had tried to invade Buenos Aires twice in the eighteenth century and failed, and we learnt about the heroic people of Buenos Aires defending their city from the invaders). The Nicholson children would be the British army, I would play the cowardly Spanish viceroy and Monkey would be Liniers, the brave general who led the improvised (and in our case imaginary) troops. The Nicholson children were rounded up by blowing on a whistle. Mrs Nicholson, their mother, had been advised by the doctor to use a whistle instead of her voice to call the seven children across the garden. One blow on the whistle summoned the eldest, two the next one, until she reached the seventh. But the children would never agree on how many times the whistle had blown, and after a while their mother would have to scream the name of the wanted child as loud as she could.

Once, coming back from downtown with my parents, I found Granny deep in conversation with Monkey. She was telling him about the time when, as a young girl, she had set up a theatre and produced classical Spanish plays, and she suggested Monkey should try the stage.

'You have a talent for acting,' she said to him. 'You shouldn't waste it. You could use all you enjoy in games and playing jokes, pretending. That's theatre, I know. I was Don Juan's Elvira, I was the Queen Isabel, I was the Princess in *Life is a Dream*.'

Same day, 4 p.m.

Now everything English is abominable, we're told. The enemy. Did I tell you that my school was an English school? It was a 'boys' only', St George's, and not far from the house. I could have walked there but my mother thought it better for me to catch the bus; she feared the foggy winter mornings which she said had crippled her brother, so a red and blue school bus picked us up every morning at seven. I enjoyed the short ride, looking out of the window at houses waking up, longing to travel away, far away, imagining every new street to be another country where people did things in different ways. School was fun. We had English in the morning and Spanish in the afternoon. A Scottish school-

9

master, Mr Campbell, taught us English literature. I still remember him jumping onto the desk and fighting the army of moving trees that was supposed to end the reign of King Macbeth. He made us learn by heart all sorts of bits and pieces: Byron, Keats, Emily Dickinson. Even Auden: 'If equal loving cannot be, let the more loving one be me.' His father had come to Argentina with the English company that built the railroads (which is why in Argentina the trains run on the left track) and he loved this country like he said Hudson and Cunninghame Graham had loved it. 'You,' he'd holler while the wet blackboard rag hit us strategically on the ear. 'May we be brought into the confidence of a brain you no doubt consider superior and share the latest idiocy it has managed to hatch? Let us all have a taste of that *viveza criolla*, "native wit", which you seem to have acquired in these vast austral regions.' And after the culprit had stammered some excuse, he'd mimic great pain and continue, for the benefit of no one in particular: 'God in His infinite wisdom has put one of the richest and most beautiful countries on earth into your jam-smeared paws. Not now, but in fewer years than you can imagine, the decisions and the laws of this land will carry your names. And because I don't want you to be like the wizened, bitter, incapable vizirs who are now in charge of the job, I will work your heads to the bone boring the way for some wisdom. And now, I believe our friend has something to tell us about this subject. Open your Stevenson on page 104 and read. It's meant for you, you herd of gaping llamas, so rejoice in it.'

When the weather was fine he'd troop us out onto the football field and tell us a detective story or if it was raining and he felt bored with Shakespeare, he'd pull out a tattered anthology from his hip pocket and read out Kipling's *Danny Deever* or Chesterton's *Lepanto*, where 'the walls are hung with velvet that is black and soft as sin, and little dwarfs creep out of it and little dwarfs creep in.' We loved it, and the soul of Danny Deever rumbled over us in the skies that he had never seen.

You see, to us these people we are fighting *are* what stood for civilization. This is a war against the Romans. Together with *'Las Malvinas son Argentinas'* we were taught to dress like Englishmen, to behave like Englishmen, to play sports like Englishmen. Americans were imperialists, the French were lusty and dirty, the Italians and Spaniards 'the necessary soil from which we sprang': but the English were civilized, did nothing that wasn't cricket; they had the style of living we aspired to. And then, suddenly, you were the pirates, invaders, barbarians. The day the English are defeated we will stand in our Burlington Arcade tweed suits, hold our glass of Scotch whisky in one hand and our roast beef sandwich in another, and proclaim that the Empire's days are over.

Samuel, snoring by my side, cares little about the fate of either country. His vast, dry land in the North is the only country that's real to him, and it does not belong to either you or us.

Tonight I will try and dream of that first night with you in Paris: of the tea getting cold in the red cups on the table, of Gormenghast jumping off the bed with a dignified shrug to curl up near the cupboard door, of a faint smell of cinnamon and ginger lingering in the air, of voices in the courtyard shouting a name and laughing, of the pale, soft winter light filling the windows and the room, spreading over the carpet and the table and the bed, waking us to the skeleton of a tree tapping against the frozen panes in the early morning wind.

Thursday, 13 May 1982

We're hungry. Breakfast was *maté cocido* (again) and soggy biscuits. Lunch (if we're lucky) will be some kind of soup. We're terribly hungry. Some of the soldiers have been down to the houses and begged for food; some got it, most came back with nothing. Jorge, who was studying to be a lawyer, whipped out a pistol at some farmers and came back with cooked lamb and bread and green peppers. He wasn't caught, but he won't try it again. Rules are strict. In the

11

other battalion a soldier tried killing one of the sheep and was found by his sergeant. He was made to pull off his boots and stand in freezing mud for over an hour. It is absolutely forbidden to kill the sheep. We are supposed to be 'civil' to the kelpers. Why? The officers have enough to eat, they don't care.

This morning I woke up to a day-dream of smells: I could distinctly recognize fried eggs, toast, coffee. That first morning when you thought I was still sleeping I watched you get out of bed, so beautifully naked, lift Gormenghast from his corner, get him some milk. I watched you light the burner, break the eggs, make the toast. I wanted to hold you from behind and kiss you, while the smell of the food mixed with yours on the pillow, and then I wanted to sit with you and touch you while we ate. You brought the tray to the bed, sat cross-legged, naked like a statue, and I kissed the crumbs off the corner of your mouth, and followed the line of your hair down your shoulders with my finger, bright against the snowy background sun. (My mind has formed a picture of you, as clear as a photograph, as motionless, as unchangeable.)

That morning I told you about my brother. You, without brothers or sisters, have always had your parents to yourself alone. You said, 'I never minded being an only child: I loved coming back from school or playing with my friends and knowing that this was my corner, mine alone, and that there was nothing to share, nothing to give up.' Perhaps that is what now gives you confidence, makes you so sure of yourself, so wonderful to talk to. You never seem to need more than what you have. You're so beautifully contented.

I've always hankered after attention like a drug addict. I loved then (I love now) your calm, detached way with things, your silent but happy mood which makes it clear that you do nothing you don't want to do, you say nothing you don't want to say; the world's worst diplomat, that's what you are – and I need you terribly.

You asked me about my brother and first I thought I wouldn't tell. But then, as in a dream, I felt it didn't matter.

Being with you was like being on a long transatlantic cruise. It didn't matter much what I said or did or thought; this mirage would last for however long, and then would vanish, a dim memory, a vaguely familiar face. Suddenly I felt this wasn't real, you weren't real, and the room and the snow and the cat weren't real – and that nothing mattered at all. I talked. I told you about Argentina. I told you how Argentina's military government had allowed Perón back into the country; Perón the dictator who had plundered Argentina for years under the pretence of being popular, and who then, after a long exile in Spain, had been invited to return and stand again for presidency, invited by the same gang of bastards who had kicked him out for their own convenience years and years ago. So he came back; he came back with his wife Isabelita (a cabaret dancer whom he had picked up after the death of his first wife, Evita); he came back with his secretary, an astrologer called López Rega who would read the liver of pigeons before giving government advice; he came back with his pet lap-dogs whom he would take for walks around the block every morning, giving the journalists something to snap at.

'The worst is still to come,' Father would say. 'But then we'll have the calm after the storm. The good old days will be back.'

'Back?' Granny would answer. 'You can only take *that* much beating and tearing to shreds. Bleed a country once, twice, but in the end it will give up. I'm too old to have hopes but not too old to care. We used to say that countries have the leaders they deserve. That's not a compliment to my grandchildren.'

'Please, no politics,' Mother would shake her head. 'It is awfully bad for the digestion, and anyway, I don't like these things discussed in front of the children.'

'I said what I said for the children,' Granny would snap back.

'Please, please,' Mother would wring her hands.

'Well, we shall see what happens when Perón does come

back. Things can't be worse than they are now.' Father liked to have the last word.

The day Perón arrived started with confusion. He had promised to land at Ezeiza, the international airport, and the people (the blind, conservative, star-crazy people who had been so much abused by him and by all dictators to follow) flocked out into the open to greet him – men, women, children – in trucks, cars, buses, on foot, on bicycle, in thousands and thousands. And then, just before the plane landed, the shooting started. Some say it was Perón's men, trying to protect him from an imaginary assault; others say it was the military government, trying to create a last-minute confusion. The result was hundreds of wounded, many dead, everyone bewildered, aghast, and the hero of the day Perón himself, who landed at another airport, safe and sound.

I was waiting for my father at the hospital when the first ambulance arrived. No one knew exactly what had happened, or why. I remember a middle-aged woman dressed in grey, carrying a small child, wounded, in her arms. She startled me with her very calm voice, asking: 'Why did this happen? I don't know why this happened. Can anyone please tell me why this happened? We were only going to see him arrive; we were so happy he was back. At last.'

The guerrillas, who had kept the military government at bay for several years and almost forced it to bring Perón back (they believed that what was popular was good) then tried to make a pact with him. They failed because he betrayed them, and after shaking their leaders' hands in his own house he established the fiercest reign of terror Argentina had ever experienced. The guerrillas attacked again and again; paramilitary troops invaded the city and counterattacked. Not a day went by without someone, left or right, being kidnapped. People were shot dead in the streets in broad daylight; no one was safe. If you were on someone's list, in someone's phonebook, you'd be arrested. No trials, no lawyers. Just arrested and killed. Age, sex didn't matter. Children were hauled off with their parents; friends and relatives were tortured and killed.

Of course the university was in an uproar. My brother was eighteen then and had just entered the Faculty of Engineering. Did I ever show you that building in Buenos Aires? It was built in the shape of a Gothic cathedral, with thin grey columns rising to form arches above the door; high, ghostly windows and broad winding staircases. The top was never built because the architect realized too late that the ceiling would never support it, so now it crouches like a flattened spider, looking through its slit-like vertical eyes at the throngs of students below. At the time it was plastered in posters and graffiti; groups of politicized students broke into the classes and made speeches; spies listened in on every lecture and professors and students disappeared without trace. I knew that Juan was part of some liberal group and that he went to meetings somewhere downtown (all political meetings – in police jargon, all meetings – were forbidden). He knew little about politics but soon realized that studying under those conditions was impossible. I think he became part of a group out of frustration, out of the sheer need to do something, even though he didn't know exactly what. A friend of his, Raúl, whose grandfather had been in the Spanish Civil War, used to lend him books.

Friday, 14 May 1982

Samuel said this morning that Perón was alive somewhere in the North and would come back when the time was ready. Will Perón become our King Arthur, a deformed and grotesque modern version of the Sleeping King? Juan's friend Raúl kept saying that the people couldn't be wrong. If they wanted Perón, Perón was right for them. Monkey's comment was:

'The people also wanted Hitler.'

Juan would launch into long explanations as to how the

'course of history' was determined by the 'people's will'.

'And who are "the people" you so freely refer to?' Monkey would ask. 'I am the people and I don't want Perón in the government. He smiles too much, like Count Dracula. It's not a pleasant smile.'

Juan, Raúl, Oscar and other friends would meet and discuss politics. I admired Juan: I admired his freedom, I admired him for coming home late – he had his own key; I admired him because once a girl, I think her name was Silvia and she had beautiful red hair, phoned him and invited him to her party, and he turned her down. I would have given anything to be have been invited.

His face, his figure come back to me sometimes, but not his voice. For a long time after he disappeared I tried to remember his voice. I felt I had betrayed him, forgotten him, destroyed the little he could have left by letting that part of him which was mine, his voice, fade away.

Our first Christmas morning in Paris I tried to tell you about his voice. We sat over the eggs and toast and I told you about that time when I became afraid of the night. Our large house in Olivos had many rooms; the bedrooms were upstairs and each of us had one to himself. Mine was small, at the very end of the corridor, looking onto the back yard. One night I felt I wasn't alone in the room. I was about eight at the time and as I lay there I let the feeling grow into a certainty: something else was there, lurking. I wished Rex, our dog, were with me. But mother made him spend the night in the kitchen. I felt that something was moving behind the red curtains, then among the books on my shelves, then under the bed, beneath the pillow, crawling onto the blanket. I was terrified, too frightened to scream. I just lay there, trying to close my eyes, trying to tell myself that it was nothing. As I lay there incapable of moving, the door suddenly opened and my brother came in. He saw me, looked surprised, and then just sat on my bed and talked. He talked and talked – I never really remembered what he said – but his voice cleared the air and soothed me and whatever it was that had scared me disappeared through the solid walls. I remember how he went on talking and talking and how I felt myself drifting off to sleep, his voice like a soft rumble in the background, guarding and protecting me. When he disappeared I tried to recapture that night but couldn't; the images were there, but like a screen with the sound switched off, his voice had vanished.

One morning we realized that Juan had not come back home to sleep. My father called up a few of Juan's friends; after speaking with Raúl he phoned the police. But long before that we knew. It had happened to so many people, we knew exactly but said nothing. I can see my mother, sitting under the large portraits, staring into the air; Granny moving from one room to the other as if she could find Juan hidden in one of them; my sister Ana crying in the kitchen. Two weeks later my father got hold of his friend the Archbishop; four hours later we were travelling south in a train from Constitución. Father had wanted to travel alone – his doctor's bag, his fine poncho which he wore as an overcoat had been laid out ready for several days – but Mother wouldn't hear of it – the portraits of her ancestors were there to remind her of her duty – and of course neither my sister nor myself wanted to be left behind. Granny simply took it for granted that she was going. Dusk was falling as we left the station, the carriage full of singing campers and crew-cut conscripts returning home. The journey was long and dusty: the pattern on the seats has fixed itself in my mind, grapevine stems crawling through the tiny red bristles of velvet in the first-class compartments, all thinly coated with dust. I also remember a black-and-white photograph of Lake Nahuel Huapi staring at me from the wall opposite. We reached our destination at four in the morning. Red-eyed and stiff we staggered onto the platform. A solitary soldier had come to meet us, either for security reasons or because the Archbishop had specifically requested it. He showed us into an army jeep and we set off again through the sketchy town of low white and pink houses while day was breaking across the horizon.

What you call the pampas is nothing: a thin black line

between the earth and the sky, uninterrupted and slightly curved; a solid bare sea, what someone called 'horizontal vertigo'. Suddenly a red square building became visible next to a clump of trees. We drove through a guarded wooden gate and miles of barbed wire. We were greeted by a short officer with lacquered hair and a black moustache. He shook everyone's hand, invited us into his office and drew up chairs for the ladies. He spoke to my father, 'as a father himself and as a fellow-countryman', he shook his head at the 'unfortunate turn of events'; he regretted the 'misguided fires of youth'. Then he said he would have Juan called in. Five minutes later the same soldier who had brought us from the station came into the office holding Juan by the arm. My mother let out a stifled scream. Juan's hair had almost disappeared: a few strands stuck to his scarred skull as if he had suffered from a serious skin disease. Short dirty bristles gave his whole face a grey look. His eyes were bloodshot, his cheeks drawn in. An ugly cut ran down from his left eyebrow almost into his eye and over the bridge of his nose. When he put out his hands we could see that his thumbs had been smashed: they looked black and blue and enormous. The nails had probably fallen out but I couldn't or wouldn't see. My mother stood up, uncertain as to whether to touch him. My father threw his poncho off and tried to hug him, but Juan gave out a yelp, like a dog. The officer made a few apologetic remarks about my brother having got 'bruised' in a scuffle. Then he said he supposed we wanted to be 'private' with him. He wasn't allowed to do this, he pointed out, it was 'completely against the rules of course', but 'there now, he understood'. He called to the soldier and then left us alone. My father opened his doctor's bag and started dressing my brother's wounds. My mother just stood there, making noises in her throat. I almost asked her to stop. Ana was crying; Granny sat and said nothing. Slowly Juan put a hand inside his belt and drew out a piece of paper, muttering something. It sounded like 'I'm sorry'. My father put it away in his bag. The officer came back escorted by two other soldiers, and Juan was taken away. The meeting had lasted barely ten minutes. The officer said he hoped everything would 'sort itself out very soon'; it was clearly, he said, a 'misunderstanding'.

As we walked out a couple of soldiers came into the building holding the arms of a large black-haired woman; they held her up so high her feet barely scraped the ground. She looked at us, once, and was jerked away. We had to wait two hours for the next train home. Father asked if we wanted to eat something; next to the station was a small grocery store that served coffee. Each of us had a cup. As I sat there I thought of the woman carried away by the soldiers, and wondered whether anyone knew where she was.

Saturday, 15 May 1982

When you read about wars, when you see them in films, the action lies there, in front of you, like a detective novel, clear and unravelling, following clues, connecting this army to that, this face to that general, this move on that day. Here, now, in the midst of it, we know nothing. We have lost track of the fighting: we are never alone. The shooting carries on day and night, but we no longer know who is shooting whom. Mysterious lights still cross the sky but we don't know where they come from, what they mean. We are now in a ditch some soldiers have dug out. It's quite deep and muddy; the walls are slippery and white, splattered with a kind of grey fungus. Beyond stretch the hills, dull, foggy and greenish, with milky streaks like a disease of the rocks. The sky, in contrast, is brilliant blue, very clear. Last night, almost without us noticing, it stopped raining.

One of the groups on the Two Sisters came back last night. There had been an explosion and most of them were hurt. I was told to help unload the wounded. I crouched next to one lying there, with his back turned to me, and I tried to hoist him onto the stretcher. As I pulled him back, his head rolled towards me: he had no face. Something had blasted it away

19

and there were only shreds of skin and blood and two large white bulbs staring at me from the mess. He opened what was left of his mouth; blood was spattered over his teeth. He tried to talk; he moved his tongue but made no sound. I managed to put him on the stretcher. After that I was violently sick. 'You can be sick later,' the sergeant yelled at me. 'Now get on with it.' We kept on loading the wounded onto the stretchers for almost four hours. Someone was calling 'Mama, mama' like a baby.

Our pilots come back with stories of the devil being on the English side. They say the bombs fall and hit the British ships but will not explode. They say the bombs are jinxed. They say the ghurkas have brought witchdoctors with them. They despise the ghurkas and call them mercenaries because they say they are fighting for a land that isn't theirs. Drugged up to their eyeballs they race down from the hills and never stop to even look at their dead comrades. What do these mountain men think of this place? Is it as alien to them as it is to us? Penguins. Penguins, sea-lions, seals: to us these were animals we went to see at the zoo. Now the penguins waddle in droves down by the beach, among the rocks and the foam. Alvarez, also from Buenos Aires, was down at the beach a few days ago: he says the stench is unbearable. It's not the penguins, it's the sea-lions. What do the ghurkas make of the sea-lions, the penguins? What will they say about these islands when they go home?

Our pilots say the English spray our planes with salt so as to frost up our windscreens and blind us. Many have crashed. Sometimes at night I think of the pitch-black sea, deep, deep down, where the sunken corpses are eaten away by tiny blind creatures crawling across the slimy sand. One of the pilots told me that his most terrible nightmare as a child was falling into the sea alive, sinking through the icy murky waters, and lying there rotting, to be eaten, clawed at, gnawed at, among other living carcasses and hollowed skulls.

Writing about the war in April, during those first days of confusion and surprise, the Argentine correspondent in

London for *La Nación* called this 'the postage-stamp war'.
He said it was a coup mounted by Argentine philatelists to
prevent the British from issuing a 150th anniversary stamp
for the Falklands. Here the talk is about Galtieri and his
government trying this war as the ultimate tactic of survival.
I'd like to be like Wells' sleeper and wake in another
hundred years and discover what historians have written
about us. Your Wellington said that 'all the business of war
was trying to find out what you don't know by what you do.'
We are the worker ants, driven and blind.

Sunday, 16 May 1982

Today we heard that the Marines destroyed an ammunition
and fuel dump on Pebble Island. No one will say how many
died. We do nothing all day: suddenly we are called out to
march, we are taken away, made to dig trenches, then
carted back. The sergeants seem to add to the lunacy of this
war by giving lunatic instructions. This morning our
sergeant said: 'If the enemy attacks from that way' –
pointing to the right – 'run this way' – pointing to the left. I
can hear you laughing. You and your sensible head planted
sensibly on your shoulders. I can hear you laughing at this
madness which is not my own, which isn't ours.

I think it was when we got back from seeing Juan that the
idea first struck me: maybe we weren't supposed to understand why things happen, maybe this whole damn thing is
the answer to a question we will never know. Granny's
solution for madness was always order.

'When it thunders I darn my socks,' she used to say. When
mother would decide to go into one of her moods and brood
or argue about everything, Granny would get hold of a
duster and a broom and undertake a vast spring cleaning.
The first thing Granny did after we got back from the
South was to go straight into the kitchen and start baking.
We all sat there, trying to find small things to do, hoping
Mother wouldn't burst into tears. From the kitchen came

the smell of warm bread, comforting. It was a smell of long ago, when we were little and Granny would bake bread as a special treat, to eat with the quince jam she made herself. Mother used the jam for tarts and small *empanadas* – which you sweetly call Cornish pasties – but Granny used to say it was too good to be put into service, that it should be eaten pure. The smell and the memories made me feel as if I were asleep, secure in a sleep where other things took place, far from Juan and the South and the prison. Father wasn't sitting. He stood next to the fireplace, staring at something in the distance, very quiet. Then suddenly, as if remembering something, he opened his bag and pulled out Juan's note. He looked at it and then at me. I came up to him: all that was written on the paper was a number. Father went to the phone and dialled. A recording told him that the number he had reached was not in service.

'What about Raúl?' said Ana. 'Maybe he knows.'

I raced out and caught a bus to Raúl's home. But Raúl hadn't any idea as to what that number could be. He promised he'd try to find out. I asked him if he thought Juan would come back. 'I doubt it,' he said. 'I'm sorry, but I've seen so many go like that. You were fortunate, you saw him. At least you know where he is. Even if you don't see him again you'll have seen him once, you won't spend nights and nights wondering, thinking, imagining the hunt and the capture and the beating. You will have an answer. There are thousands who don't even have that.'

I went back to school determined to fight. Fight against those who had destroyed my brother, fight so that something else might be made out of this country. I was fourteen years old then, and the whole world seemed terrible and grey. I felt all sorts of urges, wanting to do untold things, discover, find out by myself what the wide universe was about. That summer one of the teachers – his name was Laffont – decided to take a group to camp in the mountains down south. He was a young man, funny and intelligent; we liked him, which was more than could be said for most of the other teachers. The school was dependent on the university and for that reason we got a number of celebrities from the university itself. Professors with all sorts of degrees taught us chemistry, literature, history, music, Latin. . . . Very few taught us anything worth knowing. I remember a bulky lady with exophthalmic eyes who bore the name of a brand of cigarettes and who spoke incomprehensible Spanish in an effort to teach us physics. Such was her fury at her own incompetence that at the end of term she gave every one in the class the lowest mark: not one of us had, according to her, passed the final exam. Another character was a drunk and bloated ancient history professor who had decided that Plato had never existed and that the proof of his non-existence was in Plato's own work. We sailed from one hour to the next, bored out of our minds most of the time, back and forth from the horrors of reality into this haven of asinine knowledge. Laffont tried timidly to refer the facts of our recent past to the happenings of the present; he let us draw sly conclusions which we felt were our own; he showed us other ways of looking at things; he made us feel alive and with a brain. Twelve of our class joined his camp, and seven of the class above us. Our destination was a lake about fifty miles south of the town of Zapala where Welsh farmers had settled about half a century ago. We arrived at Zapala in the early morning and from there started walking. The Southern Andes are said to be the most beautiful mountains in the world. Unlike the eastern part of Patagonia, the West, the long frontier with Chile, is green and blue and purple. I have often dreamt of taking you there, to that dusty road we followed with our knapsacks on our backs, the fields growing greener, the forests fuller, wild strawberries shining from under their leaves as we went by, flowers with Indian names blooming on strangely-shaped bushes and the song of unseen birds calling from the deep. And in front of us, when we lifted our heads (which wasn't often) the water-coloured Andes, snowcapped, a line of ever-higher dominoes standing in our path. The air was so clear it hurt to breathe.

After a long, long walk we reached the lake, like a sea caught in between mountains. White sand like flour covered

23

the beach, and the bleached bones of dead trees, pale and smooth like naked lovers, lay everywhere in heaps. Red trees, *arrayanes*, dipped their red roots into the crystal-clear water and, during the day, unless the wind was blowing, the silence was complete. No birds sang around the lake.

At dusk, however, the mosquitoes and the crickets began their evening noise. We built a fire on the beach and watched the moon in the lake behind the flames. We sang songs then but when you and I sit there we'll be quiet and listen. Behind that lake is another, and then another, and we will go to one I haven't seen before and make it ours.

How I longed for someone to love then, on the shore of the lake, at night. Or during the day, when we brought back bread freshly baked by a Welshman's wife, and spread it with the local rose-hip jam, when we climbed the wild cherry trees to pick the cherries and found they were too bitter to eat, when we climbed the hills around us looking for the trails made by the deer, when we drank the icy water of the springs that ran down from the melting snow, I longed for a hand to hold and the warmth of another body and hair, cheeks, lips other than my own. Laffont read to us around the fire, stories by O. Henry and Bioy Casares and Maupassant and Chekov, and we learnt the songs of the Spanish Civil War and the French Resistance and the Italian Alpine Army. 'Comrade, whenever you fall, another will spring from your tracks,' and 'If I die bury me under the mountain, under the mountain.' We thought we were very brave.

When I returned I felt the horrible shame of realizing that throughout that summer I had not thought of Juan; rather, I had not thought of his death. His image once or twice flitted across my mind or through my dreams, but the rest of the time I took in the savage beauty of the South and felt sorry for myself because I had no one to share it with.

Before we caught the train back, Laffont did something none of us ever forgot. He said we had seen the beauty of the place and that was certainly ours, a part of the world we had inherited. But there was another side to it, and that also was part of our world. Behind the town of Zapala is a little stream, and crossing that stream a sort of gulch running in between two walls which used to belong to a quarry. He took us there, leading the way. As we walked we noticed, in the walls, dark openings like caves. Then it dawned on us that these openings had pieces of cloth hanging in front of them, sometimes straw mats instead of curtains. And then, slowly, shyly, faces began to appear. Thin, dirty faces, women, men, children, all looking old and sad. Laffont said that these people lived here summer and winter, they were known as 'the people of the Stream'. They were too poor to buy materials for a house and the government gave them nothing. When they could, they worked for the railroad or for the local farmers, the Welshmen or the rich landowners from Buenos Aires. We knew about the landowners; in history class we learnt how the Menéndez-Vetti family had paid, in 1935, two pesos for every pair of Indian ears 'to rid the land of vermin'. Bounty hunters and the army exterminated them south of Buenos Aires. But we had never heard about these people living here in caves today, a few miles away from all that beauty we had just seen. The contrast was too sharp, too striking. Slowly we walked back, silently. That night, in the train, I told Laffont I understood. At least I thought I did. He said nothing.

Monday, 17 May 1982

Did you realize, that very first morning in Paris, that I had fallen in love with you? Did you understand why I kept pouring out my life story to you, words and words and words, as if I needed you to know at once who I was and what had happened to me? You dressed while I kept talking, you cleared away the breakfast cups while I kept talking, you threw my clothes at me laughing and told me to dress while I kept talking and even before I knew it we were outside on the icy street and you took my hand and slipped it into your pocket with yours. We walked slowly down back towards the river, past shops and cafés closed on Christmas Day, through a city that seemed deserted and left to the hazy cold. We passed the red brick archway where Pierre Curie had been killed by a passing carriage and where Marie Curie had knelt on the pavement picking up the remains of her beloved husband's brains; we crossed the Pont Neuf where the last of the Knights Templar was burnt at the stake and where, through the flames, he called upon the King and the Pope to meet him in Hell in exactly a year's time, and the prophecy came true when they both died twelve months later; we entered the Place Dauphine which the poet André Breton called the sex of Paris because the tiny street that leads into it forks out into a V. You knew so much, you were so full of stories. I talked about myself; you didn't have to. You were aware of yourself, and happy. You talked about the rest of the world.

You said you had a surprise in store for me and led me through the gilt gates of the Law Courts into the tiny courtyard of the Sainte Chapel, the Chapel of the Kings. We entered a small room with red walls decorated with the fleur de lys and the royal initials. I liked it, but was surprised to find that this was all; it must have shown on my face because you laughed. Then you told me to climb up one of the narrow and steep staircases built into the corners of the chapel. I climbed, encased inside a tube of stone, and then, after several turns, I came out into the upper level. A forest of light seemed to explode before my eyes. Climbing the high walls of this section, high into the vaulted ceiling crowned by the meeting arches of dozens of giraffe-neck columns, rose hundreds of thousands of glittering coloured pieces of stained glass, blue, yellow, green, but mainly red, gushing like blood and roses up and down the room, an impossible vision. Somewhere an organ began to sound, the chapel filled with solemn, deep music, and the changing light from outside twinkled and filtered over the walls of glass. We stood there for a long while: you told me about the lower floor being the part of the chapel reserved for the king's servants and this the royal chamber into which the king and his family arrived through a bridge from the other building. During the war, you said, every window was taken down, every bit of glass was labelled and wrapped up, and the whole mighty construction of colour and light was buried in a safe and secret place until peace returned.

While we sat at one of the few open cafés and sipped hot chocolate from heavy white cups I made up my mind to stay in Paris with you, not carry on the tour with the unbearable tourists. I'd have to meet them on the last day to go back with them to Argentina, but that left us one whole month of happiness. I was afraid you might say no. But you didn't. You agreed quite naturally; you didn't seem to mind, you seemed even to enjoy the idea. I was so much wanting you to love me. You, however, had your work to do: you had to go about your churches and museums, you had to attend courses, you had to study at home. I promised I'd be as silent as Gormenghast if you let me lie by your side as he did and if you'd stroke my hair as you did his.

All that month Paris was ours. In the evenings we went to the Cinemathèque to watch marvellous old films for a few francs and then eat sausages and chips in a smoky bistro; or we'd walk up to the Place du Tertre and listen to the musicians play their guitars and then have a hot wine. During the day I'd follow you around. Together we saw the wild sculptures in the Musée Rodin; together we found Degas' tiny bronze dancer in the Jeu de Paume, and Cézanne and Monet and Van Gogh; together we looked at the large eighteenth-century paintings in the Louvre where mighty waxen-like figures stood beautifully dead in scenes frozen from history. In the Louvre you told me about Leonardo's Holy Family, about Freud's theory of the jealous mother, St Anne, and the swan-shaped robe that holds a hidden meaning in the picture. You told me about the young Raphael and how he had wanted to stir the world into reason, about Delacroix and his search for a true human body, about Ingres and the quiet sensual lust. And when you were not working we'd walk along the barren Tuilleries where once a palace stood and was burned to the

27

ground, and across the Place de la Concorde past the Hotel Meurice where Salvador Dalí lived surrounded by his admirers, and into the Champs Elysées guarded by white marble horses. On cold, sunny days we'd walk the streets between the Seine and the Boulevard St-Germain; we'd look into the little shops that sold everything from antique dolls to Peruvian dresses, we'd inspect the art galleries and Mr Fishbacher's bookshop, we'd pass a friend of yours who sold etchings – a tall Dutch girl who had married a Russian in order to get him out of Russia, and who now shared her tiny apartment with him and seven cats.

We even went up the Eiffel Tower together: it seemed unreal, that great monstrous iron construction, an exaggerated imitation of the millions of tiny Eiffel Towers that crowd every single souvenir shop. From above, through the mist, we saw Paris all white, and I took your picture as you leaned against the barrier in your woolly hat. I wish I had that photo with me now. I miss you. I miss you terribly.

We are moving camp in a few hours. Snow has begun to fall but it is so different from our snow in Paris. I was happy then, nothing mattered. Now the snow is just cold and wet, and cuts into the cheeks and hurts my nose and lips. Samuel, poor Samuel has got pneumonia. He kept breathing in the snow for hours and hours last night and now can hardly speak: a low rumbling sound comes from inside him, like an overworked engine. He lies here (the hospital tent has been dismantled and taken God knows where) wheezing and clutching at his medallion. The sergeant comes in and shouts that we must get a move on. I push my things into my knapsack and wait. Again, just wait. For nothing.

Wednesday, 19 May 1982

We've moved. We now overlook a rocky field and we can see the water. Yesterday I felt too exhausted to write. I talked to Jorge, the tall, clever law student from Buenos Aires. I haven't told him about you. I haven't told anyone here about you. Can you understand what it's like to have everything taken away from you? Our Professor Laffont, for instance. A month after we got back home from camping in the South, Professor Laffont was dismissed. No explanation was given but rumour had it that he belonged, or had belonged, to a left-wing organization. A few teachers protested but nothing changed. We, the students, tried to stage a demonstration. Banners were put up and a petition, asking for Laffont's reinstatement, was signed by two-thirds of the school. But we never managed to deliver it. The day of the demonstration a police van was parked outside the school and several uniformed guards armed with machine guns stood on either side of the gates. The new headmaster, installed expressly by Perón's wishes, stood at the top of the stairs, smiling.

It was during that time that the chief of police was killed. A bomb exploded under his bed, blasting his body and injuring his wife. It seems that a school friend of his daughter's, barely sixteen, had been invited several times to the house and often spent the night there. One evening, after having been asked to stay, she suddenly alleged a forgotten family obligation and asked to be excused. That night the bomb went off. The girl had planted the bomb under the bed and then disappeared. Had it not been the chief of police she might have managed to escape. But her victim was too powerful. She was found a month later: her arms had been ripped out of their sockets. One of the papers called her death 'a just vengeance'.

Studying was a risk in itself, and anyway not much could be taught. As soon as a book on a subject was suspected of being 'subversive' it was brought to the headmaster's attention; in most cases the guilty party was fired. Many teachers left the country and found new jobs in the States or Europe. Paris became an Argentine refugee camp.

Ana, my sister, was seventeen when Perón died. Isabelita, who had been vice-president, became head of the country. This hysterical, ignorant woman, advised by the same astrologer who had advised Perón, would come on television and weep her way through incomprehensible speeches. The country, once again, was bankrupt. Violence reached its worst peak ever. Tommy, Ana's boyfriend, asked her to leave the country with him. But Ana wouldn't. She felt it was a cowardly thing to do; perhaps she still thought there was some hope.

We never again discussed politics at home. After Juan's disappearance we tacitly agreed not to mention his name and dinners were quiet affairs, quickly got over with. Only Granny from time to time forgot the unspoken rule and began to remember – her memories would gush out, as if the past was too strong for her.

Granny would start: 'Perhaps we should lay a plate for Juan as well. Maybe he'll come home tonight.'

We tried not to answer, talk about other things. But Granny would carry on. 'Juan always likes this dish. He says it tastes sweet. I don't think it tastes sweet, do you? But then Juan always says funny things, doesn't he?'

Or her dreams: Granny's dreams were part of everyday life. 'Last night I saw Juan, as clearly as anything, standing by my bed. He looked cold, but not unhappy. In fact, he was smiling, you know, that funny way he has of smiling and making just one dimple on his left – or is it right? – cheek. He was smiling and I can't remember if he said anything. Probably not, or it would have struck me. Probably not. Perhaps that means he'll be home tonight. I really don't think he should be out this late.'

Granny would sometimes lose her sense of time completely and talk about us as if we were still little. She remembered Olivos when the streets had cobblestones and every winter the streets would flood and large planks had to be laid from side to side for people to cross. She would talk about her world in the twenties and thirties as if it were there, now, just outside the door, waiting for us in black and white like films on television. 'I took you' – she'd say to Ana – 'I took you in the buggie yesterday, and how you liked it! You laughed and pulled at the reins and the coachman got awfully cross; he's so jealous of his horse. But mind you, getting cross with a child, what is the world coming to, I ask you.' And she'd shake her head and drift away again. She'd talk about the political figures of her time and about the 'very refined' English family, 'really English, you know', who had moved in across the road: for fifteen years the Nicholsons had lived there, and she talked about them as if they had moved yesterday.

'I'll wear my blue silk dress again tomorrow,' she'd say. Or, 'You must tell cook to boil the *dulce de leche* for at least another hour – it was quite "undone" this morning,' and we hadn't boiled the jam at home for as long as I could remember. But her mind had slipped back to a time of slow watches and long hours in the kitchen, afternoons in the garden sipping *maté* and evenings by the radio listening to the well-known voices of her favourite comedians, all of whom were now dead. Granny made Mother uneasy.

'I don't like her to go on like that,' she would say. 'I'm sure it's not good for her.'

Father would say that it was of no importance. But Mother would insist: 'It's undignified. We must be dignified, if nothing else.'

Ana and I talked a little about what to do with ourselves, but never discussed our political activities. She told me about Tommy's plans and I tried to convince her that it was the right thing. Tommy had relatives in Brazil who could help them set up there; I was certain Father would understand, and if he gave his consent Mother wouldn't object. But Ana said she wasn't ready.

Tommy and Monkey lived with their parents in Belgrano, not far from downtown, in a small, uninteresting house, one of the few that had survived the surge of apartment blocks. Their father, Alfred Cohen, was in the leather trade; he and his wife had come to Argentina from Germany in 1939, a month before the war, and still spoke Spanish with a strong accent. Tommy had a shock of red hair and could play the violin – both legacies from his grandfather who, it seems, had played in the Berlin Philharmonic. He would take us sometimes to the Colón, Buenos Aires' large opera house,

31

and there, standing in the topmost balcony, he'd follow the time of the music with his hands. Monkey had his brother's red hair but not his musical talents.

Monkey always laughed at my brother's secret ways, and about our taking life so seriously. We forgave him because he was Monkey – he seemed to live in a constant happy state of mind we weren't allowed to reach; he, for some mysterious reason, had been granted that blissful privilege. One of his favourite tricks was to take books out of the local library and add his own comments to the text. He'd write out new paragraphs and paste them inside, changing famous, well-known writings into hilarious masterpieces. We all thought he'd be a writer, but he said he didn't have the patience. He enjoyed the swiftness of a joke, the mad fun for its own sake. That, in our country at that time, was a mark of genius.

I remember he once wrote an entire new canto to be inserted in our best-known 'national poem', the *Martín Fierro*, the epic of a gaucho who escapes from military service and roams the pampas in search of adventure. Monkey's canto made Martín Fierro decide to run for president: because he had all the attributes of a scoundrel, he succeeded. The poem played with Perón's better-known characteristics and the sleazy prostitute he fell in love with was immediately recognizable as Isabelita.

Then, one day, we heard that he'd been arrested. An anonymous phone call informed his mother that he had been taken in and that he was going to be put on trial. Monkey was fifteen, my age, at the time. The Cohens rushed over to the Central Police Department. A certain judge of minors had decided that 'a trial wasn't worth the State's money' and had sent Monkey to reform school. We tried to see him there but were told that they had never booked him. According to the officer in charge, he had been given orders to deliver Monkey to an unspecified section of the Central Police Department. According to the Police Department, Monkey had never been seen there. The reformatory knew nothing. A few days later we were all in Monkey's house, trying to think of a way of finding out what had happened.

Suddenly the bell rang and Mrs Cohen went to open the door. Her scream brought us out in a flash: Mr Cohen, Ana, Tommy and myself. There on the step was a small huddled body, naked and covered in purple bruises, hardly recognizable if not for a shock of red hair. Around his neck was a thin black line like a collar: a nylon thread was embedded in the skin. His bloated tongue peered through his split lips. His eyes were mercifully closed. He seemed incredibly old. Mr Cohen held his wife, who was shrieking and shaking. Tommy and I pulled in the little body. As Ana closed the door she noticed that someone had painted a swastika on it. We called the police. They came: an inspector and two plain-clothes men. They asked questions, took notes, shook their heads. The police doctor was quick and advised about funeral arrangements. Less than twelve hours after we found him, Monkey was buried in the Jewish Cemetery of Liniers, on the outskirts of Buenos Aires.

Thursday, 20 May 1982

I had always thought that in the end one could do anything one really wanted. I always thought that when things are driven to their very last consequences, when everything is put on the scales, when truly and logically we set all the facts before us, nothing can stop us from following our heart's desire. And even now, though I know I'm here and can't reach you, I still believe the same: that with just another effort I could get what I want, you, and that the world would be ours. We are sitting now around the fire (it is night-time) because the tents are too wet to use; we sit here while the fireworks go off as usual in the background, and the echoes of shooting and explosions and whistles clog the air. We sit here, I know, but I can only think of things far away, of a certain night in Paris, you standing there in a darkened room, lit only by the yellow windows of the house opposite. I see you smiling and I come close to you and put my arms

33

around your neck and kiss you. I comb my hands through your hair, moist with the smell of snow, and take your lips inside my mouth like fruit. My hands slide down to your waist, slide under your sweater, slide upwards and their cold touch makes you jump, until they take on your warmth, become part of you. I kiss you again, I take your breasts in my hands, I lift your sweater and bend over and bury my head against you, my mouth trapping the tip of one breast, then the other, my teeth holding them ever so slightly, my tongue racing around them, building their shape inside my mouth, making them mine. You take my head in your hands, making me stare at you, inside your eyes, dark in the dark room, your eyes full of the glimmers from outside like candles in an attic. I pull myself away, then clutch you against me; I hold you, my face on yours, inhaling your hair, the skin of your neck, and we go down, while Gormenghast jumps away, disdainful. Your hands undo the buttons of my shirt, I try to kick off my shoes, struggling with the sleeves behind my back, a prisoner, and you bend over and put your mouth hard against the zip of my trousers, biting at me through the cloth. I wrench free from the shirt, pull off your skirt, my trousers. Still kneeling in front of me your breasts now graze my knees, I kneel as well and now, on the floor, I hold you down, my tongue tracing the shape of your breasts, under your arm, over your shoulder, my teeth following the line from your neck to your elbow, my mouth taking your fingers, one hand, then the other. I lift you to your feet: I want to look at you, tanned in the yellow light from across the street. I crouch in front of you, pull you towards me and bury my face between your thighs while my fingers trace the curving line behind you down to my mouth on the other side. Then we lie on the floor, you roll me over on my back, you climb over me and make me enter you, deep, deep inside, while the blood beating in my temples seems to explode behind my clenched eyes.

Darkness comes back, the sound of gunfire and shouts

beyond the hills, the sound of machine-guns searching for something in the shadows.

Later

The question that kept haunting us was: Why had Monkey been arrested? That was what none of us could understand. Involvement in politics was certainly a secret business, but not to the point – at least we thought – that neither his brother, nor Ana, nor I, would ignore it completely.

'He must have been in it!' said Ana. 'He must have been in it!'

'But I would have known, or at least suspected,' I argued. 'It would have come out in little details, a conversation, in blurting out something about the school or the government. . . .'

'Not necessarily,' she said. 'You only see what you're looking for. For all your politics, Enrique, you imagine your own reality.'

Tommy said nothing; he looked sick and feverish. You know, after a time you learn that everything can be accepted up to a certain point. It is then that the nightmare breaks and gushes out into our safe daytime life. That little bell that tells us that we are only dreaming seems broken; we no longer can stand aside and say: 'This is only a dream; I'll wake up and it will be gone.' Reality is too powerful, it takes up all the air. Tommy felt as if he couldn't breathe.

'If I listen to you long enough, I'll go deaf,' he said. 'If I stare long enough at one point in space, I'll go blind.' And then: 'I'll wipe out my senses; I won't talk or smell or feel again. I'll never sleep again.' And when Ana put her arm around him he let out a low, sobbing howl as if a sudden pain had just then shot through his body.

I had images of Juan changing faces with Monkey, like masks, and then I saw both bodies, lying together like dead meat on a slab. The night after the funeral a light, cheerful rain fell on Buenos Aires; Tommy dreamt of puddles of mud on his brother's grave, Ana of Tommy, and I of my open window and my wet textbooks and what would I say in school tomorrow.

Friday, 21 May 1982

Jorge told me this morning that your Task Force is attacking from all sides. Now even in the daytime you can see flares. And smoke, of course, like special effects in a circus. Wherever we are, we feel surrounded. Jorge is convinced that to destroy the British will be an act for which humanity will be thankful.

'All empires die, my boy,' he says. 'Haven't you read your Bible, your history books?' He proceeds then to list fallen empires, including the Aztecs and the Mayas. 'The true reason, my boy, is sex. The Egyptians did it with their sisters, which as everyone knows today, you shouldn't. The Romans did it with everyone. The Spanish did it with sheep. And the English don't do it at all: they just like to get whipped, a trick they pick up at public schools. If you didn't know that, dear Enrique, you have a lot to learn.' I can't understand how Jorge managed to get through university.

Ana couldn't. She wanted to study psychology, but her years were the worst the university had ever known. As soon as she entered she discovered that, for example, Freud was a forbidden author. Freudian theory had been replaced by something called 'Science of the Spirit', a medieval mishmash of teachings judged innocuous by the military minds. Tommy and Ana used to meet in a little café about a block away from the university. Soon they got accustomed to the police coming in and asking everyone for their papers, intruding and probing, frightening the students into believing that the slightest hint of culture was wrong. Ana would come home in fits of deep depression and just sit around and do nothing. Father tried to interest her in his own side of the medical profession, took her with him to his surgery in town, and to the hospital. But nothing helped; the air we breathed was bleak and to Ana, more than to myself, there seemed to be no future.

'You'd be a good surgeon, you know,' he'd say to her.

'Nonsense,' was Mother's reply. 'My daughter doesn't want to mess around with blood and goodness-knows-what.'

Throughout this time Granny kept a brave spirit going. She flitted about the house, fragile as a bird, suggesting little changes, cooking splendid meals that filled the house with happy smells, talking about the time when we had all been little children, a time that seemed as far away as in a fairytale. She hadn't forgotten. She hadn't forgotten either that idyllic past or Juan's disappearance; she hadn't forgotten Juan's face in prison or the officer's smile or the silent train ride home. She never used to leave the house now except perhaps to take a walk around the block, past the flowered gardens and the English hedges behind which people like us played croquet or had a barbecue. One afternoon, however, around teatime, after Mother had laid the table with ham sandwiches and *alfajores* (those cakes filled with milk-jam, brown, as sweet as treacle, which you used to wolf down), we noticed that Granny wasn't there. We looked for her in the room upstairs, we went out and asked the neighbours. At last we saw her coming down the street from the station. She was wearing her best coat and a little cap with feathers which I had never seen her wear before except in an old photograph. We ran to her, asking where she had been. 'To Plaza de Mayo,' she answered when we were inside. 'To Plaza de Mayo.'

Every week, the mothers and grandmothers of people who had disappeared would meet outside the President's offices, the Casa Rosada, the Pink House, on Plaza de Mayo, and silently walk in one large circle around the small pyramid erected there to commemorate the Day of Independence. One of the mothers, having had no answer to her enquiries about her son, decided to come back to the square every Friday; other women joined her and their gathering became a symbol. (Later on, Friday was changed to Thursday because the journalists had pointed out that

37

Friday was the day on which witches were supposed to hold their covens.) Granny had watched their gatherings on TV and read about them in magazines. Then, all of a sudden, she had decided she'd join them and ask about Juan. She had carried her ninety-odd years to the station, she had got on the train to Retiro, she had walked up the steep hill of Plaza San Martín and then down all the way to Plaza de Mayo. There she had joined the other women; there she had marched around with them, wearing like the others a white kerchief tied around her head over her feathered hat. Some women were praying, some were silent, a few were helped along because of their many years. Granny proudly told us she had walked alone. When the demonstration was over they dispersed, peacefully, and Granny had come back. We gave her tea, we hugged and kissed her, we told her we loved her. Next morning, when Ana went to wake her with her drink, she said she wasn't feeling strong enough to get up. That day and the next, for nearly three weeks, Granny lay in the bed getting – it seemed to us – smaller and smaller, blending into the sheets with her pale pink skin, her thin white hair, her watery blue eyes. Most of the time she slept, and when she woke she would call us as when we were children or drift away to an older, larger house, a house by then demolished, a house with a sunny patio and chequered tiles and a well, a house with creepers covering the walls and long barred windows that almost touched the street. Once, upon waking, she asked me to be happy; another time she said she just wished the end to come swiftly now; it seemed tedious, she said, nothing interesting in an old woman dying. She died one afternoon, when the lights were being turned on and the curtains drawn for the night. I found her and went to tell Mother. Mother looked at me strangely, went downstairs and carefully, one by one, turned each of the ancient family portraits against the wall, never saying a word. Then she went to her room and when Father came home and tried to talk her into coming down to eat something, she locked the door from inside and started singing an Andalusian song she used to sing to us in bed at night when we made up excuses for not going to sleep.

> Antonia, of Camborio's clan
> That have blue manes both thick and strong,
> With olive skins, like moonlight green,
> And red carnations in their song.
>
> Beside the Guadalquivir's shore
> Who took your life, who could it be?
> The four Heredias, my cousins,
> The children of Benamejí.

The song lasted for hours; at last we woke to silence in the morning and the men from the funeral parlour came to take Granny away. Only then, when the black van had left, Mother opened her door and stepped out. She looked for Father, hung onto his neck like a little girl and cried.

Saturday, 22 May 1982

They say that we sank another of your ships today, the *Ardent*, but God alone knows if that's true. I can't bring myself to care. I thought of nothing but you. Remember our last days in Paris? The day before my departure you said your Dutch friend had invited us to tea. I was angry: I wanted you to myself all day, I wanted an excuse to stay in Paris, I wanted you to hold onto me and beg me not to go; I hated the calm, happy way in which you behaved even then, a few hours before my departure. I wanted you to say no, you needed me, I wanted an outburst of silly, wonderful, unspeakable things. Instead there you were, asking me to have tea with an outsider and her cats: I was furious.

Mara's apartment was on the Quai Voltaire, through a heavy green carriage door, across a cobblestone courtyard and up four flights of grubby steps. It was tiny: two small rooms cluttered with her collections: Art Nouveau drawings, 'pompier' paintings, china bric-à-brac, glass boxes, papier-

mâché trays with Chinese motifs, piles and piles of magazines, photographs in gilded frames, bits of tapestry draped
over everything. And cats: seven cats in a small apartment is
always too many. There were cats on the table, cats in every
chair, cats on the carpet, cats on the sooty window-sill and
cats in the kitchen sink. Mara's husband, the Russian she
had helped to escape, was called, predictably, Igor. He
was a small man compared to towering Mara, and hid his
dislike of cats and bibelots behind an air of sleepiness which
seemed constant. Tea was poured from an octagonal silver
teapot into octagonal silver cups; the tray was made of bits of
looking-glass that caught the many lights of the silver set.
Igor passed cream cakes around while seeming to stifle a
yawn. Then Mara said she wanted us to see something.

A couple of Russian ladies, now of a very advanced age,
had brought her something to sell. At first they were
reluctant even to speak about it, but now it seemed they
needed the money and they had agreed to part with their
most precious possession. They had come to Mara for
advice; they knew about her saving Igor and about her
fondness for curious objects. The ladies had known the
widow of Prince Felix Yusupov, the famous Russian
aristocrat who had murdered Rasputin. Yusupov had tried
to poison him. When the poison didn't work, he shot at him,
stabbed him, tried to throttle him. As if possessed by the
devil, Rasputin refused to die. Finally Yusupov managed to
drown him. It was known throughout Europe that Rasputin
had seduced every woman in the Russian Court: whether
Yusupov bore him a personal grudge for assaulting the
woman he loved is not known. The fact is that after seeing
Rasputin dead, Yusupov drew out his knife and cut off
Rasputin's all-too-famous penis. This was the object which,
shrivelled and black, lying in its velvet container, the two
old ladies had come to offer Mara and Mara was now
showing us. I will never understand why Mara decided to
expose the relic; I know that it changed my mood, its
incongruity breaking through my anger, this ridiculous
witness to history preserved for the astonishment of future

generations. We left Mara's apartment laughing and walked across the bridge: a red sky cut out the domes of the French Academy and the Île de la Cité. Flat barges and brilliantly-lit tourist-boats sailed up and down the Seine and loving couples walked across the quais as in postcards. I made you promise you would write, that you would tell me everything you did, and I'd save up money and come to see you in Cambridge. I dared not make more plans for the future: you knew what you wanted, you always did what you wanted. I felt happy at last, but also deserted. I knew I'd be very lonely, and even miserable without you. I tried not to think more about it as we walked back and up towards your Rue des Boulangers, to our last night together in Paris.

'I won't come to the airport,' you said.

Somehow I knew you wouldn't; I even hoped you wouldn't. I imagined the people, the luggage, the man at the passport control – everyone intruding. I wanted us to be alone.

'We'll say goodbye here,' I said. 'I'll start writing to you on the plane.'

'Please don't,' you laughed. 'Enrique, you have to go back, I have to study here and go to Cambridge. We'll write when we have things to tell each other. Wait a while.'

Gormenghast lay fast asleep on the bed. We had coffee and bread by the window, and then it was time to go.

'OK, I'll wait for your letter. Unless I've got something to say that can't wait.'

I'll stop writing now. The tent is flooded and Samuel is trying to get our things outside, but as it's raining it will make no difference. Jorge has come to offer us blankets. He probably stole them from someone and we are bound to be blamed. Jorge says not to be such puritans. The rain keeps falling.

Sunday, 23 May 1982

Still falls the Rain –
Dark as the world of man, black as our loss –
Blind as the nineteen hundred and forty nails

41

Upon the Cross.
Still falls the Rain . . .

More victories, they say. Now it's the *Antelope*, it seems, badly damaged. I wonder how old the British soldiers are. We are all between eighteen and twenty-five; Monkey would be my age now, twenty-two. I can't imagine him here. Sitting in a soggy trench, looking out towards a fading horizon, encroached by noise. He would explode in here, he'd clown his way out, run, shout, and get killed.

After Monkey's death, Granny told Ana to forget. Ana plunged as best she could into university life. A few professors, weary of the restrictions set upon their teaching, began to organize courses in private at home, giving lessons in secret like early Christians in the catacombs. Ana used to tell me about those classes in the evenings, how they all had to put on conspiratorial airs and go in individually, or at the most in couples, so that the porter would not suspect a meeting in one of the apartments. The effort of attending these classes and the responsibility involved made them more interesting, and they all studied hard, but Ana could not understand why they were forbidden, what the subversive reading of, say, a Melanie Klein could be in the minds of the military leaders. Obscure Catholic perversions and a thirst for power seemed to be the only guiding principle. Whatever their motives, they managed to throttle our culture, our civic rights, in the time that ran from Perón's first government to now, Galtieri's Falklands War.

Ana, helped by Father, attended certain sessions at one of the hospitals, and for a time she thought she had been able to pull through in spite of everything. The director of the psychiatric ward was an Italian woman, Gena Di Segni, who had come to Argentina with her husband in the sixties. She had an international reputation and her studies of certain adolescent problems were considered definitive. Soon after Ana had begun to attend the hospital, Dr Di Segni took her under her wing. I don't think it was my father's influence: rather she recognized in Ana a certain passion, even a certain genius which she liked. Ana mentioned her attentions to me and I felt truly proud of my sister. Then one day a group of men in civil clothes entered the hospital brandishing machine-guns. While two stood by the door, three raced up the steps to the psychiatric ward. Ana was there. She said the patients began to scream, knock their heads against the walls, run up and down the corridors in fright. Dr Di Segni came out to see what was happening. The men rushed at her, punched her in the face, and when she fell to the floor, bleeding, they took her by the hair and dragged her down the stairs and outside into their waiting car. It was all over in a few minutes. Ana says that she, like the others, did nothing. Doctors, nurses, attendants – everyone just stared in horror and fright and incomprehension at the attack and no one did a thing. Only the patients in the psychiatric ward continued their wailing and screaming, their beating and running around, till the nurses managed to calm them down, and a heavy sobbing replaced the noise. Ana says she just stood here, unable to understand. She didn't understand what had happened, why Dr Di Segni, why she, Ana, hadn't moved to help. It wasn't fright, she said, in her case, it wasn't panic. It was numbness. Nothing mattered any longer.

That evening she and Tommy talked about it for a long time on the sitting-room sofa. Next morning, when I woke up, Ana was packing. She told me she and Tommy were leaving the country for good, they were going to Brazil to start over. Mother heard us, came in and pleaded. Father tried to explain to her that it was for the best: he understood. But Mother would not be comforted. She went down to stare at the backs of the portraits which she had not allowed to be put right since Granny's death, and she stood there hugging herself, rocking back and forth, back and forth, while Ana kissed her, and opened the door, and stepped outside, while she got into Father's car and he drove her away, while I tried to talk her into coming back upstairs and lying down. She just stood there rocking back and forth, hugging herself as if her heart would break. Rex moved around her, licked her shoes and then lay down in front of her, waiting. When Father got back, she was still there.

As we waited for the world to cave in, Jorge convinced the sergeant to let us loose in town. We had until midnight. I asked him if we would take Samuel along.

'No, the kelpers don't like niggers,' was Jorge's comment.

I ignored Jorge and proceeded to convince Samuel. He could see no point in leaving camp, sick as he was.

'To do what?' he kept asking.

'To see life, if it's still there,' said Jorge.

I told Samuel a change would do us good; fresh air outside a sodden tent and maybe some real food.

'And a nicer face than the sergeant's kisser,' added Jorge, 'God bless him.'

Samuel agreed and we set off, filthy, tramping towards the lights. Jorge proceeded to salute every sheep we met on the way, 'to impress the native population', as he put it. From time to time the sky lit up with a purple hue and hundreds of little white flares blossomed and fell.

'They're celebrating my birthday,' explained Jorge. 'Every young lady on these God-damned rocks has had her fill of penguins and is aching for my body. They're throwing a fireworks birthday party to impress me.'

We reached the first houses quickly. The pub was lit, 'business as usual', and one or two farmers were hurrying in for a drink. I was about to go in when Jorge stopped me.

'No, kid, tonight's on me. I'll take you two children to a place for grown-ups.'

No further explanation. Samuel laughed. Jorge seemed to know his way because he walked on another fifty feet or so and then turned sharp left. The yellow lights that hung above the main street no longer shone down this side-street; it was pitch dark. Only when the flares hit the sky could we see the puddles we had just stepped into and the frozen pads of sheep-dung here and there.

'Don't expect the road to Paradise to be wide and paved with gold,' said Jorge. 'A little courage, gentlemen, and we'll reach our destination. Samuel, I hope your knickers, if you possess such a piece of clothing, are clean.'

The proverbial red light hung above a sunken door. I couldn't back away – I'd never be able to live it down – but Jorge's idea of a 'fun night out' was the last thing I felt like. He pushed both of us down two steps and opened a thick wooden door, into a large room lit with fluorescent tubes and surrounded by columns and doors. Three or four benches stood along the walls; two women in pink night-dresses were sitting next to the entrance, eating sandwiches. Another, thin and dark, walked about in a red bathrobe. Jorge went up to her, pointed at us, and the woman laughed. As Jorge walked away towards one of the doors the thin woman came up to us.

'You,' she said to Samuel, 'you go over there and ask for Mercedes. You,' she took me by the arm, 'come over here.'

Samuel trotted off like an obedient dog; I followed the woman to a corner.

'Wait here,' she said, pointing to a chair.

I sat down. The two women by the door were giggling. One began to pick bits out of her sandwich and throw them at me. A door opened and the thin woman came back, bringing with her a young girl, not older than sixteen or seventeen.

'You'll like her; she's English but she's OK with Argentines,' she said.

Then she pulled me to my feet, laughing, pushed us both into a small room, and closed the door. The room was bare with the exception of a stool, a plastic bowl full of water, a picture of the Argentine hero of the Independence, General San Martín, and an iron cot with a striped mattress. The girl began to undress.

'Wait,' I said.

I asked her to sit next to me. She didn't seem to

45

understand, so I spoke to her in English. At that she seemed very frightened. I asked her name.

'Helen.'

I asked her not to be afraid, I said I would only talk to her. I told her how we had got here and how we thought this war was crazy and how we all wished we could go back home. I told her I had an English girlfriend; I told her about you and how we met and how much I wanted to be with you. She listened carefully.

'We were told you would all come and kill us. We were told you would take us and make us do all sorts of things and then kill us.'

'Who told you,' I asked, 'who said that?'

Everyone. Everyone it seems had said that to her: the farmers, the shopkeepers, the soldiers. Everyone had told her that the Argentines were savage beasts who would come and murder this poor girl, and she had sat there waiting for the final shot or the blade. She came from Wales; her family had brought her over as a baby. Her father had died and her mother had been unable to get the proper papers to go back to Britain. Then her mother had died and her sister married a rich Chilean who had taken her back to Santiago. Alone she had found this a fairly easy way to make a living. She didn't complain. Mrs Sullivan (I gathered that this was the thin woman's name) was nice to her and the men who came to see her were kind. We talked and then she asked me if I didn't want her to get undressed. I said no, and we talked some more. Before I left she asked me if I would pay her anyway. I did and went out into the street. Samuel was there already, smiling sheepishly. We waited for Jorge but it was late and as he didn't show up we left. Walking back Samuel said he didn't know that they did it here the same as back home.

'It's really the same, you know,' he said. 'More expensive here, only.'

Later that night, as I was dozing off, Jorge came over to our tent and shook me.

'I expect no thanks for a lovely evening from a blockhead,'

he said, 'but kindly satisfy my ego by telling me you never expected something as grand as that.'

I obliged and he went away, contented.

Tuesday, 25 May 1982

Today is the anniversary of the Declaration of Independence: 25 May 1810, when the people of Buenos Aires stood in the rain outside the Cabildo on Plaza de Mayo and declared themselves free from Spanish rule. Here on the base we had extra rations of chocolate and the National Anthem.

> Hear, O mortals, the sacred cry:
> Liberty, liberty, liberty.
> Hear the sound of broken chains,
> See noble Equality on her throne.

Mother always considered 25 May a celebration in bad taste. To her, Spain was the home of her ancestors, and she never felt certain that independence was a good thing. After Ana left she seldom left her bed. Sometimes she'd get up, wander down the stairs in her nightdress, look at us and without saying a word, go back to her room. Suddenly the house was empty. With Juan, Ana and Granny gone, Father and I sat alone at the big table staring at each other over the silver candlesticks. He would try and talk about his work and I would try to listen, but the effort began to tell.

'All this is rubbish,' he'd say. 'All this will pass and things will again be as they should always have been. In my days, as a student, I used to manage on ten pesos a month. With that I bought my books and ate and went out and bought my suits. Everyone had work. No one went without meat not once but *twice* a day. Chicken was for the poor – if there were any. Liver, kidneys we gave to the dogs. That's how wealthy we were. And then Perón came. When he said he could walk on the gold stored in the Treasury he was speaking the literal truth. He could. We were a rich, civilized country. Once. And mark my words: we'll be one again. We must be patient.'

I tried to argue, a little. I tried to ask him how; how could one bring a country back to its time of so-called glory, once it had been dragged through the years we had just passed. But to my father this was the nightmare; reality had just been suspended and with the Grace of God all would be back to normal. One evening, as we were sitting there, both of us, Mother came down and lit the candles on the table. Father asked her not to, said it wasn't necessary, but she just smiled.

'I'll take them to my room,' she said. 'I need light.'

We saw her climb upstairs, her nightdress waving behind her in a ghost scene from a black-and-white movie. Then the door slammed. A while later the smell of burning reached us and we ran up to her room. All her dresses had been piled up on the floor and she had set them alight with the candle. While we were stamping out the flames she sat on the bed and said,

'You shouldn't worry, it's just that I won't wear them any more.'

Then she put her arms around my father. Father shrugged her off, motioned me out of the room and closed the door. I waited for him to come down again, then took the dishes to the kitchen. Finally I went to my room, followed by Rex, and fell asleep. Next morning, by the time I got up, Father had left for work.

From that day onwards Father tried to stay away from the house as much as possible. Once he told me he would sell the house; it was too big, he said, for us three.

Mother stayed in her room. The cook would bring her her meals and Rex would keep her company. One evening she called me upstairs.

'Dear Enrique, I think you'll have to take the dog away,' she said. 'He's sick.' Rex lay on his side, with his tongue out, gasping for air. I carried him down and called the vet. He came to see him at once: he was an old Scotsman who had helped Rex's mother deliver her litter and had offered us one of the tiny puppies. He looked him over and said there wasn't much he could do. He thought Rex had been poisoned.

I told him it was impossible. When Father came home Mother had locked herself in her room again and the vet had taken Rex with him.

Next morning Father called me into the study. He had packed a couple of suitcases and had tied up several of his books in small parcels. I could hear Mother singing in her bedroom. I asked him where he was going.

'I'll live in the office from now on.' (He called the surgery his office.) 'I'm leaving now.'

'What about Mother?'

'She'll be better off on her own. She'll keep the house, everything. But she'll be better on her own.'

He waited a moment and then said, almost as an afterthought, 'You'd better come with me. The office is big enough for both of us.'

'But who'll look after her?'

'A nurse. I won't have her put away. But I can't stay here either.'

A small woman with dishevelled black hair appeared at the door of the study.

'This is Soledad. She knows exactly what to do. Now get your things.'

I did. I packed my clothes and books and put them next to Father's. Then we got into his car and drove down to his surgery. I felt the worst of traitors but unable to do anything else.

Saturday, 29 May 1982

Today we heard of yesterday's attack. It's been four days since I wrote last but on Tuesday we were marched off to the trenches and the bombing never stopped. Last night I slept for what seemed the first time and today Jorge arrived with the news that the British had launched a parachute attack on Goose Green and Port Darwin and recaptured both positions. The sergeant overheard him and yelled at him to stop talking nonsense or he'd be reported for treason. But afterwards another soldier said that thousands of our men had been captured. Horror stories about what the civilized British are doing to the Argentine soldiers are spreading like the plague. Some say they have been tortured, others say they have been raped.

It's just barely more than a year since I left Paris – well, almost a year and a half. How long ago it seems. I left you and Gormenghast and the Rue des Boulangers and got into the plane with a sickening feeling in my stomach. I kept trying to read notices, to look at the people around me, to flick through the book I had bought in the waiting lounge. The sound of voices chattering away in Spanish made it impossible to forget that I was going back – and that you were not here with me. The plane was late taking off; the stuffy heat didn't make me feel any better, and I had finished with the magazine in my seat-rack before the motors started humming.

The lady sitting next to me – a plump Colombian matron who looked like García Márquez in drag – launched immediately into the story of her life: how she had been visiting her son, an artist, in Paris, Paris city of the Arts, but other children were expecting her, back in Bogotá, a lawyer, fine lawyer, and a girl, schoolteacher, fine schoolteacher, did I know anything about art, had I heard about whatever-his-name-was? I saw you back in Paris without me, with the cafés, the streets, the shop-windows that had been ours, and felt sick. The Colombian woman kept on talking, about her house, her husband, her cousins, how she was getting off in Rio, how she would spend a few days in Ipanema, how from there the connections to Bogotá were infrequent, how. . . . The thought suddenly struck me that I also could get off in Rio. My only suitcase was with me in the cabin. My sister was there; I hadn't seen her since she and Tommy had decided to leave. I'd stop over and see them. I felt better. I wasn't going back then, I was going somewhere else. I'd be able to talk to Ana about you, I'd tell her about us and we'd talk about the future. At last the Colombian woman nodded off and I settled down to read my book.

We arrived in Rio before dawn. As soon as I stepped off the plane a whiff of hot, perfumed air struck me in the face. There was vanilla and sugar and sea-water in the smell and it felt as heavy as fog. After immigration I looked for a phone. I hunted for (and found) Ana's number. Then, sleepy and angry, came Ana's voice.

'Ana, it's me, Enrique,' I blurted out.

There was silence. Then: 'Enrique, for God's sake, where are you?'

I told her.

'Enrique, you idiot, come over here at once, why didn't you think of this before, why didn't you let us know you were going to Europe?'

She gave me instructions for the bus; then she changed her mind (I could hear Tommy prompting in the background) and said I should take a taxi. She gave the address.

We raced along an almost deserted highway against a background of round, dark mountains. Dawn was breaking, hot and full of colours, and a hot wind blew through the taxi's open windows, filling my eyes with dust. As we advanced it became lighter and the earth redder and redder; palm trees shot scraggy leaves into the air over shacks made of corrugated iron and fruit-boxes. Thin children, black and white and all shades in between, stood outside and watched us pass. The houses turned to stone, the streets became more numerous and the city of Rio grew around us.

My sister's house was one of a bunch that sat underneath a green hill. Red hibiscus bushes cluttered the entrance and a yellow dog whimpered away as we drew up. Ana and Tommy raced to the door before I had a chance to ring their bell. Hugs and kisses, pats on my back and a hand ruffling my hair, I was almost lifted inside by both of them. Ana sat me in a vast, flowered armchair; the smell of fresh coffee came in from somewhere and a minute later

51

Tommy set a tray with biscuits and a steaming cup in front of me.

'First eat,' said Ana. 'Then we'll talk.'

Life had been quiet for them. She had found a job in a hospital and Tommy was at the university. Nothing exciting but at least it wasn't dangerous. 'To find peace in Brazil,' laughed Tommy. 'After all we kept saying about their army of torturers it seems almost a blasphemy.'

'Sometimes,' said Ana, 'I feel as if I had simply given up. I feel as if I had sat down and given up and decided that it was all too much for me. Other times it is worse. I get the feeling that maybe we were wrong. That nothing can be changed, not by speaking out or by protesting or by forming groups or by anything. That we are up against a huge invisible monster whose slaves are our generals and our politicians, a monster made of many faces and names and ideas, each moving in its own direction and each doing its stuff for personal and secret motives. And that is why we can't get at it, because we are not fighting one system or one person; we are fighting a tangle of greedy and petty evil, and when we hit at one point there are a million others that simply continue to thrive in a million other directions.'

'What we feel is useless,' said Tommy.

But I was no longer listening. I had visions of you coming to see me, back in Buenos Aires. We'd settle down together, we'd do something. Then we'd travel. Nothing else mattered. I think I fell asleep in Ana's chair.

Sunday, 30 May 1982

Samuel is one of the many who have been punished. He's on half-rations, which means nothing. The muck we eat looks the same, however many spoonfuls you dole out. Samuel's been punished for disobeying orders, orders which he never even understood. But punishments are flourishing now, like a form of revenge. And last night there was a fight. One of the soldiers – I think his name is Nicasio – punched a sergeant, and, like Samuel, was put on half-rations. I would have thought that for punching a sergeant you'd get more than half-rations, but everyone's so tired no one seems to care. He punched the sergeant because he had ordered him back and Nicasio refused to obey. It was freezing last night. There were little pools of ice inside the tent. I kept breaking it, cracking patterns in the pools while lying in my sleeping-bag. Breathing hurts, the air is so cold. When you crack the ice the light shines on the pieces, like in a kaleidoscope. It reflects the tent, broken, torn, in shreds like I imagine it will look after the attack. Because we all know the attack is coming. We know they're here at last, the British, building up, blasting light-rockets on us to take a better aim at our camps. Is this what war is like anywhere? Was it like this fighting with swords and daggers and jungle-spears, and in the trenches of World War I? Is it always like this, repeating itself, tedious, waiting, never moving, incomprehensible, dully painful, like toothache?

Someone stole socks from the supplies tent – why are they keeping the supplies locked up? For when? He stole the socks and a sergeant saw him. He was taken out and stretched on the frozen ground and straps were tied around his wrists and ankles to pegs hammered into the ground. They stretched him out on the frozen ground and left him there and we could all hear him saying, not crying, saying slowly: 'I am cold, I am cold, I am cold, I am cold.' On and on into the night, with the sizzle of the rockets and the crack of the shots in the background, on and on and on, 'I am cold, I am cold, I am cold, I am cold.' We tried to talk louder, to sing, and shout, but his voice kept going on and on. At last Nicasio ran out, said he couldn't take it any more. He ran out and started to cut the prisoner's straps with his penknife, and the sergeant ordered him back. Nicasio didn't even answer, just went on sawing at the straps, saying: 'He can't fight if he's cold, it's too cold to punish someone like that.' Then the sergeant took him by the shoulders and swung him back. Nicasio had the penknife in his hand, but didn't use it. Instead he made a fist and hit the sergeant right on the jaw.

53

Then he finished cutting the straps and walked back into the tent.

Monday, 31 May 1982

Rio is a European's Latin America. The heat, the beaches, the flowers, the fruit. If you go there one day, you'll meet Ana and Tommy. After Juan's death I realized that I still had Ana, I discovered I had never really loved her, and then she left. When I saw her in Rio we both, I think, felt the same: we had a past to share.

The thought struck me suddenly. Ana and I were walking down the black and white waves of the Copacabana pavements, the sun scorching and the air full of smells of food. Ana said Tommy had left early that morning; we had the day to ourselves. My sister looked happy: her big eyes shining, she seemed as though on holiday, in her striped dress. We walked along the *veredas* by the sea, by the beach where the *Cariocas* come down in throngs day in, day out, past the bird-like kites posed on the sand, impossibly symmetrical, a flock flown out of some ancient Indian frieze. Black men everywhere were selling hats, ice-cream, *maté*. Then Ana said she couldn't stop thinking about Juan.

'I know. There's always something I see and think: I'll tell Juan, or I must ask Juan, or show this to Juan.'

'Tommy says that some nights I wake up and sit in bed and won't talk to him. I don't even remember in the morning. He's always on my mind.'

'Father refuses to talk about him now.'

'Have you found out what that number was?'

'No. I tried again and again. But all I get is a recording saying that that number doesn't exist here.'

'You mean in Buenos Aires.'

Ana stopped. We both thought the same thing, at the same time. We raced back to her flat. We couldn't phone from just anywhere; we needed a secure place. I dialled the number I had tried so many times in Buenos Aires. It seemed now so strange that none of us had thought of Rio before. Most of Juan's friends, we knew, had fled to Brazil. What would be more natural than asking us to reach one of them? The phone rang once, twice, three times.

'*Hola.*'

The voice on the other side was gruff and didn't sound Brazilian. I can't speak Portuguese (as you know). In Spanish I said my name was Enrique and that I was Juan's brother.

'I'm Oscar,' said the voice. 'Are you in Rio?'

I said I was and could I see him.

'Sure, come over.' He gave me his address and Ana and I raced outside. Half an hour later we were at Oscar's. His flat was tiny, cluttered with bad paperback editions of Latin-American classics and Soviet translations of Marxist writers in Spanish and Portuguese. The face of Ché Guevara looked down on us from a red and black poster pinned to the wall. Dirty coffee cups were spread about the place and a cardboard box with half a slice of pizza decorated one of the corners. We sat on green and pink cushions.

'When Juan was arrested he gave my father this number, your number. It was by chance that we thought of trying it here. We thought it was a Buenos Aires number, you see.'

'There's a whole bunch of us here, some doing better than others.' Oscar smiled. 'In prison Juan gave me a letter. I was there with him. But I have a Brazilian passport, my father was working here when I was born. They said I wasn't fit to "infect" their jails. They put me in a truck and drove me to the airport. I was deported.'

'Have you got the letter?'

Oscar got up and rummaged through some boxes. He was quite fat, and from behind looked fatter because he wasn't tall. He brought out an envelope. On it Juan had written 'To the Family'. We thanked Oscar and left. I couldn't bear the thought of reading Juan's letter there; I wanted to be alone with Ana. When we got back to her flat, Ana made some coffee. Then we sat at the dining-room table and I tore open the envelope.

Dear Family: Dear Mother, Father, Ana, Enrique,
Dear Granny,

I don't know if I shall see you again, but I know that after last night this is my only chance of reaching you. There are so many things I have to say. I want to say how much I love you all and how much I want to be with you again. But there is no way out. I am certain of it now. There is no way out.

No way out. There is nothing now left for us to do. A pack of monsters has taken over our country and unless we want to let them take over our lives as well, we must fight. For me it all began as 'a different experience', something to do against the boredom, the lack of action. I had long discovered that Argentina, in spite of Perón's words, was not a country for young men. Haggard, vile, aged men had all the strings of power in their hands, and at the end of their lives they still would not let go. What we learnt at school meant nothing. Systematically whatever we were taught was either contradicted by what took place in reality or by a simple statement, 'it cannot be done'.

On the one hand, teachers and the system showed us a new world ahead. On the other, teachers and the system told us it could never be obtained. Later I realized I had joined the group because there I felt free. I was fighting for the right to talk, to criticize, to point out blatant injustices. I probably sounded Byronic; I'd rather sound Byronic than be a Hitler youth. After some time, the real danger began. We were no longer considered 'unruly brats' – now we were 'terrorists'. After Perón's betrayal, after he used the guerrillas to come back into power and then sold them, sold us, to the army, we were tracked down wherever we were and killed. All is true: all the stories they tell about people being dragged off the street, from their houses, offices, cars. All is true.

There were about twelve of us; we were at Raúl's house that afternoon. (Raúl was in my class; his father is a Communist who came to Argentina in the forties; like all

Argentine Communists he's a Conservative. Raúl's father knows nothing about our movement, he'd never approve.) There was a scuffle outside the door and five armed men burst into the room. They kicked the table over, pushed us against the wall and searched us. I was beaten, Raúl was kicked, Juanita, not yet fifteen, was thrown to the floor, shrieking. We tried to turn our heads but one of the men beat us with the butt of his gun. Juanita went on shrieking. Raúl's mother appeared; another man pushed her away and she knocked her head on the doorframe. Then we were herded out. Juanita was lifted up by the ears ('we'll treat you like a naughty girl,' joked one of them); we were all locked up in a delivery van. We were let out into a kind of garage: it was too dark to see. Then one of the men grabbed hold of two of us, took them through the door, and closed it behind him. We waited. About an hour later Raúl and myself were taken through that door. It led into a living-room. The walls were covered in flowered wallpaper, the same one Granny used to have in her room. Several other men were already there. A short, bald man sat on a sofa chewing on a toothpick; on a small table in front of him were a few papers, our school magazine, and copies of *Time*. One of the men held me tight; another began interrogating Raúl. The questions he asked seemed absurd: were the Russians instructing us? Had we robbed such-and-such a bank? Did we have drugs? After every question the man would punch Raúl in the stomach; each yelp was put down as a yes by the man in the sofa. Then he asked Raúl to give the names of the 'others'. Raúl said nothing. The blows continued. Raúl stood there and I could see he was losing his balance. He swayed under each blow, he muttered 'please no, please no', his eyes were glassy. The man on the sofa got up. Looking at me he said: 'I hope your answers are a little clearer.' Then he stood next to Raúl, carefully, like a kind uncle with a favourite nephew, he tilted Raúl's head towards him as if he were going to whisper a secret and then, like a doctor performing a routine operation, with a little sigh of boredom, he took the toothpick from his mouth and drove it with a sudden jerk deep into Raúl's ear. Raúl let out a howl of pain, wrenched away from the man who was holding him, and fell to the floor clutching at his head. Blood gushed through his fingers, splattered onto the floor, and Raúl went on whimpering and yelling for what seemed a million years. As I tried to look away another of the men kicked me in the leg. They dragged Raúl out, still moaning. Then the bald man turned to me. 'Now the names of the others,' he said, and sat down on the sofa. The bloody toothpick was back in his mouth, between his teeth. I looked at the blood on the floor and at the toothpick and at the flowered wallpaper someone had perhaps carefully, lovingly chosen. I stared at the three men leaning against the wall to my right who would probably go back home that evening after a hard day's work, home to their wives and children, kiss them, pat their heads, complain about the weather or the traffic or the film on television, and I felt it all so uncanny, so insane, I no longer cared. I opened my mouth and reeled off as many names as I could remember, names, any names: names of kids I had met, of comic book heroes, of relatives, of classmates, of teachers, of acquaintances. I don't think it was fear: I didn't care. I simply didn't care. The bald man seemed to write everything down, never looking at me. After a while he motioned to the man who was holding me and I was dragged out, and locked in a small dark room with a few others. Someone put his arms around me, trembling. I don't know how long we were kept in that cell smelling of grime and vomit. I remember being woken by the opening of a door; a guard came in and we were all loaded into another van. Raúl was vomiting blood; one of the girls tried to lay him down on the floor of the van but a large blond man hit her on the head and she stopped. We sat there, some whimpering, most of us silent. The van travelled on for hours and hours. Twice it stopped and the men took turns getting out, probably to drink, and climbed back stinking of *ginebra*. The fat blond took hold of Veronica and sat her on his knees, joking with the others. Veronica said nothing while he touched her, all the while talking to the others, talking about Veronica as if she were not alive, a dead body, a dog. I think I slept.

The prison is somewhere in the South, I don't know where. Maybe you'll find me, maybe I'll be able to give this letter to someone, and you'll find me. The officer in charge here has a favourite hobby: he likes to lay you on a wooden table, tie your ankles and wrists to the table's legs and let one of his soldiers pass the *picana* over you. The *picana* gives you an electric shock. If it is passed over your head, you lose your hair. If it is passed over your tongue, you bite so hard it drills into your teeth. One night we heard that Veronica had been killed: a soldier had let his hand slip and the *picana* had entered her womb.

A few days ago my front teeth fell out and I couldn't eat. I had a thundering pain at the back of my neck; I began to urinate blood. I fainted. They said I was pretending and crushed my fingers with their boots as I lay on the floor of the cell. They took me to the infirmary. A young Indian girl acted as nurse; an army officer was the doctor. No one ever spoke to me in the infirmary, but at least it was warm and we got food. Three days later I was taken back into the cell: it was empty. I asked the guard where my friends were; he just kicked me and told me to shut up. That night the Indian girl came and brought me my antibiotics. While the guard was talking to someone at the door I asked her in a whisper what had happened to the others. 'They were taken out into the courtyard last night,' she said, 'and shot. The little girl' – that was Juanita, the youngest – 'took a long time to die. The first bullet had just pierced her shoulder. She just cried and cried. So they shot her again, many times. Now they're all dead.' I then realized why they hadn't covered their faces: if they know you're going to die, they don't bother to cover themselves.

But all this is an excuse. There is something else. Last night the fat blond came to see me. He said I'd had a long enough holiday and that now I had to do my homework. He wanted names. I said he'd got all the names, they were all here, all dead, dead names. He said no, there were more. He just sat there, looking at me. He said he was patient. He'd wait. But he wanted names. To think of something I began to repeat Our Father in my mind, over and over. But your names kept coming up, Enrique's and

Ana's, and I didn't know if I spoke them out or not. Ana's and Tommy's and Monkey's. Then I heard Monkey's name spelt out. I heard Monkey's name and address and then I knew that the voice was my own. I tried to stop. I swear I tried to stop and close my mouth and clench my teeth, but instead I heard my voice saying 'yes' to the fat blond, 'yes' to the question if Monkey was part of the group, 'yes' to the question if Monkey had stolen arms, 'yes' to any question the fat blond cared to ask. He hadn't touched me; he hadn't hurt me. I said 'yes' and gave Monkey's name because I was afraid, because I couldn't take more, because I was not one of the dead lying on the floor of the cell which the Indian girl had seen. I was not dead and was thankful, thankful that my friends were dead and not I, thankful that the shots were meant for them, and I gave away Monkey, poor Monkey, Monkey who never even knew about these things in books and on the streets, of guns and shouts and flags, I gave him away just as I would have given anyone else away, to keep myself, my miserable self, just to live. Please, please forgive me. All. Please.

Your Juan.

Tuesday, 1 June 1982

Rain again. We have been marching endlessly, cutting through sheets of rain like mock-soldiers in an opera through large décors of gauze. It all seems so false to me, so unreal. You know those strange moments just before dawn when you lie there after an uneasy night, and your dream breaks off like water in water, faintly aware of rustling noises, uncomfortable in your arms, clutching the pillow, half-awake, half asleep. . . . 'History,' says your Joyce, 'is a nightmare from which I'm trying to awake.' Our history is a bad dream. I wouldn't mind a danger I can grasp, an obvious enemy I could recognize and pinpoint and hate. But this: today you are the enemies, you with your clubs and your books and your tweeds, and in a few months, when all is over, it will be high treason to even mention this war – the very names of these islands will be an accusation. Because it has the quality of nightmares, what is true today will be impossible tomorrow; we are not free, we are not allowed to say *yes* forever or *no* forever. We have to go on, in this rain, a soggy mind in a soggy body, moved by faceless lords who will soon vanish, retire to Switzerland, among the rich.

Remember when we sat on that bench behind Notre-Dame one evening, looking at the tip of the Ile de la Cité steering ahead of us like a ship? I told you I could believe in God but not imagine him. Imagination requires understanding, it requires the elements to build up an image, and I said I had none. To me He is a shapeless incoherent force, mad and senseless, inhuman as anything is inhuman, stone or water or fire. I believe in Him as I believe in fire and in the rain, relentlessly carrying on, among us but indifferent, unconcerned – because concern cannot be one of His qualities. Mercy, kindness, charity, benevolence, tenderness – He can feel nothing. Nor wrath, revenge, fury. He grows like a wave that crashes down by His sheer force, and we are dragged along behind, believing that when we ride the crest or are drowned in the depth there is a reason. In truth we are just carried away from wherever we happen to be, like seaweed.

Once we talked about Manrique, that fifteenth-century Spanish poet who wrote a wonderful ode to his father's death. I told you then I wished I could translate it into English for you, because the Spanish was so true and moving. This morning we stormed into a little farmhouse. The owner had left and we walked into the house out of the rain. Breakfast had been cleared and the things stood by the sink, drying. A small bed occupied one corner of the single room, covered with a patchwork quilt. A framed page from a magazine showed a scene from the Shetland Islands, with ponies in the foreground. I thought it odd that a man should come all the way from the North and bring with him his landscape, only to settle in the same landscape here in the South: it seemed a very long trip to be in the same place. We sat around, dirtying the rug with our boots. One of us began to write graffiti on the wall but the sergeant knocked the pencil out of his hands.

'Maybe you muck up your own walls at home,' he said, 'but here we'll behave like gentlemen.' For a moment I thought he'd say 'English gentlemen'.

On a small shelf I saw a few books: a collection of poems by Robbie Burns, the *Guinness Book of Records* of 1975, *True Crime Stories*, a couple of Desmond Bagley novels and Longfellow's *Verse*. I picked up Longfellow and flicked through it and there, incredibly, I found Manrique. It seems Longfellow, in his youth, translated him. One of the soldiers started singing to himself and the others slowly joined in. I sat on a bench and copied out a few lines:

> O let the soul her slumbers break
> Let thought be quickened, and awake;
> Awake to see
> How soon this life is past and gone,
> And death comes softly stealing on,
> How silently!

We learn these lines in Spanish by heart, at school. They are as much a part of us as Wordsworth's daffodils are a part of you.

> Let no one fondly dream again,
> That Hope and all her shadowy train
> Will not decay;
> Fleeting as were the dreams of old,
> Remembered like a tale that's told,
> They pass away.

I remember saying the words to you in Spanish while the Seine flowed on towards a yellow sky in the distance.

> Our lives are rivers, gliding free
> To that unfathomed, boundless sea,
> The silent grave.
> Thither all earthly pomp and boast

Roll, to be swallowed up and lost
In one dark wave.

In the afternoon, after waiting for something – anything – to happen, we left the empty farmhouse, the books, the bed, and marched out again into the rain. I don't know how many hours we've been walking like this, stopping and starting. I see your warm arms again and again while the sergeant's voice calls us from the left. We're off.

I didn't stay in Rio. I felt I had to get back to Buenos Aires and speak to my parents. Maybe because I didn't want to be left with the knowledge of Juan's confession, or simply because I needed to talk to someone. A long time ago they showed on Argentine television, in black and white, Christopher Lee's version of Orwell's *1984*. Towards the end, faced with a torture he can't bear – rats coming into a cage put over his face and eating their way to his skull – Christopher Lee blurts out the name of the woman he loves; he gives her to his torturers instead of himself. In Juan's case the torture was past. The horror, the pain, the dread that made him a child cowering in a cellar, past all reasoning and hope, was over; during a cold and private meeting he simply gave, offered, Monkey's name. I wonder whether fear could drag on, like 'fog in your throat' as Browning calls it, drifting down and into everything, filling us and our space with dull greyness, making blunt any feelings.

I see you running across a field, somewhere in that Cambridge I've never seen, full of sun and leafy trees, people with Thermos flasks lying around, buses humming past in the distance. You will be thinking of lessons, the evening news, friends. Fear of this sort is extinct in England. I imagine that during the War perhaps the planes at night, the bombs, the shattered buildings, moulded a fog-like fear – but that was long, so long ago. This is now, and here. Juan's fear has

63

spread down south, like a storm; has covered the continent, has swept across the sea and infected these lost islands, and I don't know if, when the blast comes and the shouts in my ears explode and I see the Gurkhas' knives about to enter my eyes, whether I too won't pray for someone, anyone, to take my place, to be killed instead of me. I don't want to disappear, I don't want the next day to come without me. I want you and I want to be with you, and I can't understand why this is happening.

When I got back from Rio my parents were there to meet me. Father had decided to bring Mother to live with him. He had sold the house, dismissed Soledad and the cook, and looked after Mother himself. Mother was looking well, but Father looked weary, holding her arm as if he feared she'd run away. As we drove home from the airport I wondered when and how I would be able to tell them about Juan. Instead I told them about you.

'An *inglesita*,' Mother said, 'a little English girl. Are we going to meet her soon?'

I said that you had promised you'd come to see me as soon as you could, maybe for the holidays. Summer was ending here in Buenos Aires, humid and short-breathed, and the leaves were changing colour. My parents' new flat, in Palermo, was on the fifteenth floor and from the windows you could see the park sloping down to the railroad, and the brown river behind it.

Father decided that we should discuss my future immediately. What was I going to do, would I work or would I study? A friend of his was an editor at one of the major newspapers: why didn't I go to see him? He might get me a job.

La Nación, our equivalent of *The Times*, had moved offices and was now in a solitary skyscraper near the docks. I asked for Mr Guillermo Güell, and waited. Güell, like my father, wore a poncho. He was a short man, about fifty, and his face wrinkled when he smiled – which was seldom. We sat in a small office and he asked me if I wanted to become a journalist. I said yes.

'You know,' he said, 'you will see things and then you will write them down and you will see them again. The reality on the paper never coincides with the reality of your eyes. It is impossible to make words work for you if you want to force them: follow the rules and let things fall into place; that's my advice.'

Then, warming to the subject:

'Once I was sent to report on the trial of a bunch of so-called terrorists. They turned out to be youngsters, like you, maybe twenty or twenty-one. We never heard what their defence was; they *had* no defence. They were judged by no jury, they were never heard; only the prosecutor explained their case to the judge. As you know, trials are on paper in our country. But the judge wanted this one to be oral – it gave him a chance to speak his mind. For two hours he went on and on about the sense of discipline and justice that this country needs and that if we let young thugs get away with murder the country would soon be swept away by torrents of blood – and other such metaphors. Finally he sentenced them to life imprisonment. I wrote a long report explaining the political implications of the case. They were making a *political* statement; in spite of the accusations it was never proved that they attacked or injured anyone; it was even mentioned – to the prosecutor's credit – that two of the accused were supposedly in La Plata when the bombing happened. I pointed all this out in my article and I felt I had done a good job. Next day it was printed. They hadn't changed a word, but they had published my article in the crime column, thereby making the youngsters common criminals. You don't need to write with a bias to be biased; even the position of an article in the paper can change your meaning and your sense. So don't get any brave ideas of pin-pointing justice or reporting evil. You will be doing a job, like selling potatoes, and nothing will come of it. I have yet to see a journalist causing a stir in Argentina.'

I said I'd still rather work for the paper than sell potatoes. Güell slapped me on the back and led me on to see the chief.

I wrote to you that very evening and told you about Brazil

and about my first day back in Buenos Aires. I had kept my promise; I had something to say. I remember thinking that what I wanted to say came out of me quicker than my hand could follow; I stumbled over my lines trying to reach you. I would work that year and we would meet after Christmas. Here or in England, it didn't matter. I fell asleep counting the days in the months that were left.

Thursday, 3 June 1982

Samuel received a letter saying that his sister is getting married. To celebrate, Jorge got out a bottle of wine he's been hiding and we went down to the rocks and watched the birds and the sea-lions and got drunk.

'These are our best judges, these smelly-whiskered *señores*,' said Jorge.

'I wonder what they taste like,' said Samuel. 'Their meat, I mean.'

'Great idea. We'll sacrifice one of the beasts to the altar of our interiors.'

'Even you, Jorge, wouldn't eat such muck.'

'Sir, what you so disdainfully call muck has been known to supply regal meals at the best households of Atlantis. In fact, Captain Nemo, that kind gentleman who buried himself 20,000 leagues under the sea, served it in steaks, sprinkled with tasty sperm-whale cream.'

'I don't believe you could catch one, anyway,' said Samuel.

Jorge, red from the wind and warmed by the wine, leapt to his feet. 'I'll get one for you. You can tell your sister she has been feasted with the king of the sea-beasts.'

Jorge began climbing down the steep rock, splashed with foam. We tried to stop him but couldn't reach him. Then we lost sight of him. We could hear him laughing.

'Look over here,' Jorge shouted. 'This one's got a bigger dong than mine.'

We heard a bellow and leaned over. One of the bull lions wriggled ominously towards Jorge.

'I don't think he likes you,' called out Samuel.

'I won't try to find out.'

Then the beast attacked him. It buttressed Jorge with its head, it groaned and roared, it seemed to want to bite him. Jorge howled and finally managed to climb onto the slippery rock. The bull looked at him a while and then waddled off towards the rest of the pack. We pulled Jorge up.

'That will teach you to seek nourishment elsewhere. Samuel, I wish your sister better luck in finding food.'

We were drunk and strangely happy. We started singing the National Anthem, replacing the words 'freemen' by 'sea lions' and staggered along the road back to the camp. Suddenly from somewhere on the left a jeep came shaking its way across the stones. It stopped short of the path. A sergeant put his head out from behind the splattered windscreen.

'Get in; a guy's wounded in here. Hold him down.'

We climbed in and the jeep shot off. Inside, lying on the muddy floor, lay a soldier our age. His eyes were wide open and he kept arching his body and trying to talk, but only a gurgle came from inside his throat.

'I'll hold him,' said Samuel. But he kept squirming and curving his back into an impossible position. Then the green blanket that was covering him slipped. His left leg had been shattered and the white splinters of the bone stuck out through the skin a hand's width. The whole leg was covered in blood and white, greasy tissue. Jorge turned away and was sick down the side of the jeep. The wounded soldier jumped up and down once more and then fell back, his eyes still open. Samuel was mumbling something. After a while I heard the words 'Ave Maria, Ave Maria, Ave Maria.' Then we reached the camp. We heard that in Goose Green faulty ammunition had killed a number of Argentine prisoners.

'The swine,' said Jorge. 'These, and those. These with their incapability and those with their arrogance. May they share the same pit in Hell.'

Friday, 4 June 1982

In Buenos Aires I spent my days waiting for your letter. In the afternoons I'd stroll down to the paper and work till two or three in the morning; then I'd sleep till midday. The new hours helped me get along: my day was different, it gave me a vague feeling that time did actually pass. Your first letter arrived a month later. I had sent you a dozen: long ones, short ones, filled with things that now make me blush. Yours was full of news. I felt lost. I had expected great bursts of love and promises and desperate memories. Instead I heard about your parents taking a holiday in Cornwall; I read about your old friends Hannah and Sue and William, biting my nails with jealousy – why did they have you instead of me? And your new friends, the courses you were planning to take. You wanted to study French, to sing in a choir. You even wrote about an old boyfriend, Fred, and I cursed poor Fred from the bottom of my soul. Gawky Fred, pimply Fred, riding a creaky bicycle by your side, sweating into his shirt. One paragraph I loved: you told me about your room in that house with the other girls, your bed and curtains and books thrown about carelessly. The things on your desk: a letter-opener in the shape of a fox with a blade for a tail; a postcard of Sir Christopher Wren because you love his churches; a Carnation Milk tin which you use to keep pencils in; a blue china ashtray – although you don't smoke – with marbles in it. You never asked me to give you my photo – and I haven't got yours; maybe we felt we didn't need them. I thought of you sitting there, looking out of the window onto a small lawn, while I was at the typewriter at *La Nación* in a large hall like a mess-tent, dozens of other typewriters pounding away, surrounded by men in shirt-sleeves who trotted about looking tired.

I lived with the image of your room, waiting for another letter. I was desperate for it. I would wake and wait for Mother – quieter, calmer now – to come in and say 'the post arrived' and if she didn't – almost every day she didn't – I would feel sick in the pit of the stomach, empty, alone, and would write you one of my long, sad letters, or maybe just a note which began 'No letter, again' and ended 'I love you'.

Every afternoon, before going in to work, I would sit at a small café on a corner near the paper. From Florida Street the roads slope down towards the river and the embankment where the skyscrapers now stand, but along those roads, many of which are still paved with cobblestones, are cafés of the turn of the century, manned by Spaniards whom we call *gallegos*, Galicians – for no particular reason. The windows of my café are large, the tables dark and the coffee very strong. Many of my letters were written at this café, *El Trébol*, 'The Clover', looking out at the people in the street from the cave-like darkness. My waiter, a man called José, was a Spanish anarchist who had come to Buenos Aires after the Spanish Civil War. He was a short man, almost bald, with big red patches on his cheeks. His breath smelt of garlic. Every day he'd ask what I would have and bring my small black coffee in a thick white china cup, and stand there and talk. I liked José: he only believed in himself.

'If a man can't believe in himself, he can't believe in anything,' he'd say. 'You take a woman, she knows what she's got. She believes in what she's got. She doesn't go around saying, "Look here, God gave me this pair of tits," and slapping them on the table as a proof of holy writ. She keeps them to herself until she wants to give them. Same here. I don't owe anything to anyone – not to the government, not to my neighbour, not to God. So if anyone needs anything he gets it from me because I want to give it: that's all. In the War the priests were all anarchists. "Bugger the pigeon" would be their common cry, you know. No masters, no Master. That's how you get things cracking. I remember this priest we found in a farmhouse near Alicante, fucking his balls off in a haystack with a broad so big it took you a week to get over to her bum. When we found them, the priest just smiled at us and said: "Brothers, this young Christian needed help and I gave it to her." "Well, put your help right back before we cut it off," we said. "But brothers, isn't every man his own master? Let me

69

decide when to stop," and he just went back to work on the broad. We laughed but afterwards kicked his butt all the way to Alicante. He promised we'd burn for that. "Not a bit," I said. "You can't burn in a fire you don't believe in. I'm an atheist, thank God." Now, did you say you wanted another coffee?'

José's boss was an anarchist as well and the café didn't close on Sundays nor on any of the holidays. 'Even when you don't work you need refreshments,' they would say. José's boss was a bull of a man, with a mane of black hair, black beard and moustache, like that ogre Chaplin always keeps bumping into in his films. José was a lover of poetry and he would recite the long, endless Spanish ballads, the *romances*, to me, specially the more erotic ones. 'A king had three daughters, all three were his beloved. . . . The youngest of his daughters, he took with him to bed. . . .' Or Lorca's ballad of the unfaithful wife: 'I took her to the river, thinking she was not wed. . . .'

José had saved his earnings and bought himself a small cottage by the sea, in Pinamar, where the pine forests go down to the beach and where fishing is good. He'd spend time there sometimes in winter, when the tourists were away, and live alone with the wind and the gulls. 'This is a great country,' he used to say, 'wonderful cities, nice asses and good fishing. Pity about those goats in the government.'

I never missed an afternoon at José's café. He asked me once whom I was writing to, and I told him about you. He advised me to forget the whole thing. 'Too much letter-writing, that's never good,' he said. 'Books, yes. *Don Quixote*, yes. But letters . . . In a few months you'll wish you had never put those things on paper. It would make the Virgin herself blush to see all that purple stuff set down in black and white. What you want is a good rub-down with a nice chunk of ham. And *that* you won't get in a letter.' One day he introduced me to a plump dark-haired girl, his niece. We talked for a while and then she left.

'So?' he asked me afterwards.

'No thanks, José.'

He looked at me severely. 'If you don't use your teeth they'll fall out and you'll end up not knowing what you've got them for. Always be grateful for a free sandwich.'

Then in June, when the rains had stopped and the cold set in, and Buenos Aires turned grey and melancholy, I got your letter from London. I had taken a flat of my own near the paper, imagining it big enough for both of us. It was small but full of light, even in the bleary winter days; a living-room-cum-bedroom and a kitchen. The first night I moved in I lay on my mattress on the floor and thought of you. I love new flats as much as I love old houses. I love the white bare untouched walls in the dark, illuminated by the sweeping lights of passing cars, and the impeccable ceiling. I like to think of the room upside-down, the ceiling the floor, and picture the flat that would then look so empty and vast, like a cave on an unknown planet. I lay there and pictured you beside me, like one of those moon-lit illustrations of the *Arabian Nights*. I remembered Auden, that poem you liked:

> Lay your sleeping head, my love,
> Human on my faithless arm;
> Time and fevers burn away
> Individual beauty from
> Thoughtful children. . . .

Then, the next morning, Father stopped over to bring me your letter.

I can't tell you how I felt, how sick, how alone and miserable. You tried to be kind about it. You said you had gone to London with your French professor; you said you had both slept at the house of a friend of his; you said you didn't think it would matter, you didn't think you loved him; but you said that now things were different; you said you knew you didn't love me any more; you said that maybe you loved him. You tried to be clear, and soothing; you said you wouldn't write again.

I let myself sink into my work. I sat at my desk writing up

copy, waiting to be called to go out on whatever assignment the 'bosses' chose. I was certainly the youngest among them – men of fifty or sixty who had seen too many things and written about them – and I was treated as a kind of mascot. One day after midnight, when we were sitting at the paper's cafeteria waiting for the day's edition to close, I confided in Güell. He said he was envious. He said he had once felt like that but it was long ago and he couldn't remember. He quoted by heart a poem by Borges, the blind writer whom I had seen many times making his way slowly through the streets downtown. It was called 'To one left alone'.

> The world is no longer magic; you've been
>   abandoned.
> No longer will you share the clear pale moon
> Nor the slow gardens. Now there's no moon
> that isn't a crystal of loneliness, a painful sun.
> Farewell the mutual hands and the brows
> love brought together. Today all that is left
> is faithful memory and empty days.
> No one loses, you repeat in vain,
> but that which he doesn't have and never had.
> And yet being brave is not enough to learn the art of
>   oblivion.
> A symbol, a rose tears you apart
> And a guitar can kill you.

Güell made no attempt to pacify me. 'Cry it out, Enrique,' he said. 'It passes sooner than you know and in a few more weeks, maybe even a few days you will be asking yourself what her name was.' Time the healer – that advice never helps. Buenos Aires was full of you because I had imagined you everywhere: I had thought of us together down this or that street, in this or that café, in my flat, at night, under the light of passing cars.

We are now in a trench near Port Stanley. Surrender leaflets were dropped there, we are told, by British planes yesterday afternoon. Our sergeant says there will be no surrender. I feel anxious now for an end: I am exhausted. The second time I saw Borges in Buenos Aires he said: 'The generals had taken many things from us, but at least they had left us our honour. Now they have taken even that.'

I had met Borges in August while working for the paper. They sent me to interview him because he had received yet another prize from some American university. I walked to his flat on Maipú Street, and up to the fifth floor. His maid, a small, dark woman of fifty-odd years, opened the door and led me past some curtains into a tiny sitting-room. 'The *señor* will be with you in a moment,' she said and disappeared. I looked around. On both sides of the window stood shelves full of books. On one of the walls hung a Piranesi engraving showing some circular ruins. Silently Borges came in, dressed in grey and feeling his way with his hands. The skin on his face hangs loose, and his eyes look pale and sleepy, but his voice is hypnotic. It's slow and deliberate, following his breathing, and he uses it to punctuate his sentences. He asked me to sit on one of the armchairs and he himself sat on the sofa between the two bookcases.

'Encyclopaedias,' he said, pointing at the shelves, 'just encyclopaedias. There was a time when encyclopaedias were not at all the thing to have, you know. You were supposed to read only the original works, prestige and all that. With the first money I ever earned I bought myself an encyclopaedia. The *Britannica*, eleventh edition. It was quite extraordinary . . . articles by Stevenson and Macaulay. . . .'

I told Borges I had never seen a *Britannica*. He got up, very slowly, and crossed the room to a bookshelf hidden in the back of the room. A clock ticked away to the rhythm of his walk, very slowly. Borges passed his hand over the books.

'This one, I think.'

He pulled out a volume. It was *Ba to Br*. 'Are you in it?' I asked.

'Not in the good editions. But unfortunately my name has slipped into the latest editions, or so they tell me. In this one I was mercifully ignored. I can't understand why anyone should want to know about a doddering old man.'

He shuffled back to his seat. From the open window came the sounds of the cars below.

'Age brings one comfort: you no longer try and pretend to be another. You see the day arrive when you will simply be no more. I think, you know, that that is my wish – if we're allowed to have wishes, like children at birthday parties. That this, as Macbeth says, "might be the be-all and the end-all here, but here, upon this bank and shoal of time".'

Borges went on to talk about Shakespeare, and about Stevenson, Chesterton, Wells – his favourite writers. He had a few of their books, and several others: not many for a man who lives by them. He has none of his own books.

'There exists the strange superstition that one's work should for some reason be preserved. Instead of letting time decide, we decide for time, and bind our little works in hard-back coffins.'

He smiled, and clasped his hands as if in prayer.

'In Argentina, you know, we have the superstition of being original. Instead of taking advantage of the whole world, which is ours by right, we for some strange reason prefer to limit ourselves by the Atlantic, Brazil, and the Andes, in a petty triangle. Being Argentine is an act of faith: there is no such thing as being Argentine unless you have an unlimited capacity to believe in fantastic literature.'

And then, leaning forward, as if confiding in me:

'We are alone, you know. No one is watching. There is no great eye of the Lord hovering over us. We stand for what we do and say in the bottom of our hearts. And all the rest, as Valéry wrote, is literature.'

After a few hours I said I was leaving. I had the impression of having attended a very wise, very moving one-man lecture. Borges walked me to the door.

'Come and see me again,' he said. 'Come again.'

One Sunday the editor collared me as soon as I arrived. There had been a kidnapping – not a political kidnapping – somewhere in Almagro and he wanted me to look into it. He called a photographer and we raced off in the official car. Almagro is a low, ancient suburb. The houses are squarish and sad, squatting like fat white women on pavements lined with trees. We stopped at a long whitewashed front with no windows and rang the bell. A man in his sixties, dressed in striped pyjamas, came to the door. He hadn't shaved and white bristles were sprinkled over his chin like salt. He let us into an open-air patio; behind, covered in creepers, stood the house.

The editor hadn't told me that the kidnapping had taken place among gypsies. Four gypsy women sat around a small tree sipping *maté*. A cat stretched himself and came up to me, rubbing his back against my calves. I asked the man what had happened.

'Gloria,' he said, 'damn Gloria took the girl. That comes from sending those kids to school. She's mine, the kid; Gloria's got no business with her. Now she won't give her back.'

'Have you called the police?'

'They never come to us gypsies. But if the papers tell the story, Gloria will have to move. She can't afford having her name dragged through the mud. She's got her reputation to protect.'

'What does this Gloria do? Is she any relation of yours?'

'She's my bloody wife, if you pardon the expression. She reads fortunes there, across the road.'

I decided we'd better take a look at this formidable Gloria. We thanked the man and left. The three women were still sipping away. They hadn't even looked up once.

Gloria's house smelt of dead flowers. She wore a long, flowered, gaudy dress and her hair was done up in a bun. The weight of her necklaces made her stoop and her hands

75

were heavy with rings. Gloria seemed older than her
husband. First she wouldn't open the door; then she
relented. Behind her, in the darkness, we could see the
bright eyes of a frightened little girl. Gloria took us into the
kitchen where a pot was boiling. She ordered the girl to take
it off. Then she turned to us.

'What do you want?'

We explained that her husband said the girl was his and
that she could get in trouble with the police if she kept her
here.

'She's no one's daughter, that one. Heberto just got her
from her mother, who didn't know what to do with her.
She'll go to him in a few days. But my back's out. I need
some help around here.'

We asked what she did for a living.

'The future, my boy, the future. What will happen to
whom and who will marry. Who will die tomorrow and who
will make a fortune.'

'That's illegal in Argentina, fortune-telling.'

The woman laughed. 'Illegal! Even the secretary of
General Perón did a little of his own magic, eh? And who
can say that was illegal? He used to draw the Holy Cross in
blood on the Presidenta's back. And who's to say that's
illegal? Here,' she said, hobbling towards me and holding
my hand, 'let's have a look at that legal little hand.'

She stared at my palm for a while.

'A wanker, eh? A wanker, my boy. Love gone and all
forlorn, eh?'

I pulled my hand away.

'I haven't finished,' she said. 'Long life, lots of children,
big house by the sea – well, none of that.' Then she closed my
palm. 'Can't do a thing with a wanker,' she said. The
photographer was killing himself laughing. I felt as red
as a beetroot. I tried to talk to the little girl but she ran
away.

'Tell Heberto he'll get her back soon enough. Not to
worry his ugly head any more.'

And then, just before we stepped outside once more:

'Take care, young man. Don't waste the little time you have.'

When we told Heberto he just cursed her and us and the paper. We drove back in the dark.

Sunday, 6 June 1982

Early in the morning: it's hazy and cold, as if we were encased in ice.

On 21 September, the first day of spring, I got another letter from you. Another letter telling me about the beauties of Cambridge and your studies. The difference between us, I think, comes from our countries. Your world is old and built slowly, carefully, mistake after mistake, throughout the centuries. You have been savages, you have been Romans, you have been Saxons and Normans, and you have forgotten it all, but it's there, layer after layer, in your blood. You are old and when you build a house or write a line there are centuries and centuries of houses and words behind you, propping it up, giving it the shine certain paintings have when they are painted over coats and coats of previous washes. We, instead, are here only since yesterday. Our grandparents, sometimes our parents, weren't born here. We are making our mistakes today, and having to make do with them as if they stood for Keats' truth and beauty. There is nothing else.

You can be calm, you can enjoy life with the leisure of a rich man on holidays; I have been given a few tired minutes, and in them I have to cram my life, our history and our future. Whatever you lose, you put down to experience. Whatever I lose I've lost forever. Your river flows back, again and again, each tide making it new. My river is motionless, but once it's gone it becomes part of the sea and never returns. The Thames and the Plata are different. You never really lost me because you felt you didn't have to keep me to have me; I lost you the minute you were out of my sight. I needed you with all my heart. I still do.

I wrote back what tried to be a friendly letter. My routine was now established. Every day I'd get up at midday, have my coffee at José's, go to work, come back at three, and on Sundays lunch with my parents. I talked to José a lot and one day he told me he had written a letter and would I mind enclosing it in my next 'epistle', as he put it. I was surprised, but said yes. He said I could read it. I did. It was something along these lines:

27 October 1981

Dear Miss Sarah,
    Please forgive me for imposing myself upon you in so singular a fashion but Enrique has told me a lot about you and I believe that friendship knows no frontiers. In fact, I don't believe in frontiers at all, and the day will come when they will all disappear and we shall once again be free – but that's besides the point. The reason for this missive is to inform you of the state of my friend's heart. It's a good heart: I've heard it pound away at the table of the café he likes to honour with his presence; it is youthful and can, on occasions, be happy but right now it is full of you. If you will allow an old man to be romantic I will say that it is hard for me to see a youngster like this go to rack and ruin because of a relationship he doesn't seem to understand. I take it he went to you like a bulldozer: it is my experience that it is not the best approach with human beings of either sex. My own dear wife, Magdalena (may she have filled the belly of a good-natured worm and increased the number of roses on this planet) used to say to me: 'José: I love the way you treat me; like one of your mates at a game of cards.' And Magdalena wasn't a woman to pay compliments out of habit, she being large and voluminous and the proud possessor of hair as silky as the underbelly of a Basque ewe.
    Therefore, Miss Sarah, let me say this: I know this boy, he is my friend and he is a *caballero*, and if you were to honour this humble café with your presence I'm sure he would know (thanks to my instructions) how and how not

to treat you and offer his companionship which is all anyone is entitled to offer on this earth. The day will come when we will walk shoulder to shoulder, men, women, children and Portuguese alike, no bosses, no painted idols, no laws except those in our hearts – but that day is still beyond the horizon. In the meantime there is little of interest that we can do except get into bed with a hot-water bottle or a person of the opposite sex (preferably the latter) and spend the night neither asleep nor discussing the importance of eating codfish with a spoon.

In the hope that this invitation won't fall into deaf ears, I beg to remain,

Your humble servant,

José Guillermo Valencio Ortega de Perillamas y López Velarde.

Monday, 7 June 1982

Yesterday the British took Fitzroy and Bluff Cove. And one of the sergeants deserted. He walked into the enemy lines carrying a white handkerchief, like in the movies. No one does anything any longer. We wait. From time to time we are lined up in the trenches and told to shoot – but where? We can see nothing. Clouds of smoke, noises that seem so near you can almost touch them – but nevertheless it all seems set-up, artificial. Now we know Port Stanley will be taken. What will happen to us? I wonder if during your wars your soldiers found themselves reflected in your enemy's poems; if any of your soldiers quoted Hölderlin or Goethe against the German troops who were trying to kill them. When I think of death I think now of your Wilfred Owen, and his war, maybe not too different from mine, when he says,

And Death fell within me, like a deepening moan.
And He, picking a manner of worm, which half had hid
Its bruises in the earth, but crawled no further,
Showed me his feet, the feet of many men,
And the fresh-severed head of it, my head.

The weather here is like that of Christmas in England. Everything is covered in thin snow, making the rocks and grass look airy. Even the bodies – now a few bodies lie out there, just over the trenches – seem elegant and light, touched by the snow. Our Christmases, summer Christmases, are different of course.

Last Christmas was so difficult to bear. It was hot and humid; along the embankment the jacaranda trees were shedding their lilac flowers and the streets seemed covered with paint, unreal and gaudy. Shops dressed their windows in winter scenes, Christmas trees and sweaty Santas sprang up on streetcorners and the walls were full with posters for summer resorts and ads for Christmas shopping. Father had suggested we spend Christmas Eve at the Sheraton Hotel, as there would be just Mother, he and I. I remembered the Christmas when Juan got boxing-gloves and was so frightened of them he hid them in his closet: he said he was afraid he'd kill someone if he hit too hard.

Christmas at the old house. . . . Early on Christmas Eve Granny would begin rummaging around the kitchen getting her pots together. She would prepare the stuffing for the turkey, and the tomatoes and tuna, and the wonderful chocolate-covered swiss roll filled with *dulce de leche*; Mother would be in charge of the turkey itself, and we were just ordered to keep out of the way. On Christmas Eve we ate late, very late, so we all slept our siesta in the afternoon. Then, shortly before twelve, we all got into Father's car, dressed in our best outfits, and drove to the Church of San Isidro, a small red building overlooking the river. The moon sometimes shone in through the stained glass and the organ would peal and we would stare in wonder at the golden saints and the flocks of angels on the ceiling, and the priest would announce, we knew, the birth of Christ our Lord. One Christmas the San Isidro choir sang the *Misa Criolla*, the mass sung to native music, and Granny, who had never heard it before, cried and cried: she said that it was full of the spirit of Christmas, like the songs she sang when she was a little girl.

'I'm sure that God has an Argentine accent when He is born again in Buenos Aires,' she said. 'When I was little, the angels talked to me at night in the dialect of my province; why shouldn't they be good at accents, God and His hosts in Heaven?'

Then we came out in the summer air full of the smell of flowers, and drove home to the delicious dinner and the presents.

You have your Christmas meal on Christmas Day, so you don't know how wonderful it is to stretch the night in celebration, to fill your heart with food and drink and coloured wrapping-paper. Christmas Day was enjoying the presents, but Christmas Eve was Christ's birth. We were allowed to taste the wine (wine from Mendoza – Father said that Christmas was no excuse not to be patriotic) and Ana's cheeks would go bright pink and Granny would say: 'You're glowing, my dear, like an angel's bum.'

But now, without Granny and Juan and Ana, the Sheraton would be fine. We would go to mass afterwards. The Cathedral wasn't far and they had announced a candle-lit procession.

Dinner was over at about eleven. Mother was quiet and smiling. She had even managed to do up her hair and wore a sparkly net on it that caught the lights above the table. Then we drove to the Cathedral on the Plaza de Mayo. Just outside, the Mothers of Plaza de Mayo, the same that Granny had joined, stood silently watching the people go in to await the birth of Christ. They stood there, saying nothing, doing nothing, and the men and women in best coats and dresses trooped past them, as if trooping past a knot of beggars. They watched us, heads covered by white handkerchiefs, and when we came out again they were gone. Next morning we heard that the police had dispersed them.

'They are ghosts,' Mother said as we got into the car. 'They are all dead, all dead. They shouldn't be out here when they're dead.'

I said goodnight to my parents and walked to my flat. The night was full of another Christmas, just twelve months ago, and I said to myself that those other ghosts wouldn't let me sleep. But they did.

Christmas morning I woke at about ten; I had slept for barely five hours. The day was clear and bright and cold. I decided I'd take a walk. The whole city seemed shut; there was no one on the streets and even the cafés had closed their blinds. The newspaper kiosks were covered in pale green cloths, the flower stands were empty; Buenos Aires seemed in mourning, like those Indian tribes whose mourning is white.

I walked for a while, staring at the shop windows that looked like unopened presents left over from the day before, and, almost without noticing it, I ended up at José's café.

He was there alone, wiping the tables and humming a song of the Spanish Resistance, something about Franco's wife and the whorehouses of Madrid.

'Hello kid,' he greeted me. 'Bugger Christmas! Not a soul around. Is that any way to celebrate a birthday? Where are the balloons? Where's the fun? Where's the bloody cake? If this is how you Christians celebrate His birthday what do you do for Lent? Die?'

He sat me at my usual table by the window and went off to get my coffee. I called out for a sandwich as well.

'If you don't mind bread as hard as a bishop's balls and ham so rubbery you can easily pass it off as a tinted condom, a sandwich will come up in two minutes.' I had brought with me a small anthology of poems. It fell open on a poem by John Masefield:

I have seen flowers come in stony places
And kind things done by men with ugly faces,
And the gold cup won by the worst horse at the races,
So I trust, too.

I sat back and looked out of the window. Nothing moved,
as in a picture. Behind me, José was clattering dishes and
humming to himself. Somewhere a radio began to sing carols.

Then there was someone standing next to me. I looked up.
A blue dress, a smile. I couldn't believe it. I had often read
descriptions of visions that seem impossible, apparitions
that, though they seem real, seem tangible, don't exist, like a
mirage. I never quite believed them. There seemed to me a
clear line between our waking and our dreams; we always
know when we are dreaming and when we are awake. Little
hints, little senses make it clear. For the first time I wasn't
certain. There, standing by my side, was Sarah, you.

You sat down. You said: 'I came; I made up my mind. It
was silly to be with my French professor and think of you. I
decided I'd come. I don't promise I'll stay but I'm here now.
I arrived this morning. I knew you'd be in the café.'

José came to the table, beaming. 'Is this your *gringa*? My
compliments. Miss, you don't know how glad we are to see
you.' And he shook hands effusively.

I just stared and stared. I didn't know what to say, where
to start. José came over again, this time with a bottle of
sparkling white wine. 'A toast,' he said. 'To a young lady
who doesn't believe in frontiers.' We drank.

'Let's go,' I said. 'I want to walk with you, hold you . . .
let's go home.' We went out, wishing José a Merry
Christmas, and started to walk down the street. The city was
ours: I hardly knew where I was going. I felt very drunk. In
the end we arrived at my place. It looked a mess. There were
books everywhere; dirty coffee cups on the table; the bed
unmade. Only then it occurred to me to ask: 'Your luggage?
What did you do with that?'

'I left it at the terminal. It's OK. I wasn't sure how long it
would take me to find you.'

I held you, tight. We kissed. My hands were in your hair and your hands were around me and we turned around and around as if dancing, and around again until we fell on the unmade bed, my hands still in your hair, kissing your lips, your nose, your eyes, laughing, together. When I looked up again it was dark outside. Everything was about to start.

You were here, with me, in Buenos Aires. I could take you to my parks, my streets, my corners and shops and houses. I was like Stevenson's child:

> And all about was mine, I said,
> The little sparrows overhead,
> The little minnows too.
> This was the world and I was king;
> For me the bees came by to sing,
> For me the swallows flew.

I suggested we visit my parents. You asked me to wait. You didn't want, I think, to be shown around like an exotic beast, sleek and civilized; you'd see them in your own time. I promised I wouldn't insist. Christmas Day disappeared. We went out for an hour or so, to look at the night, and then came back to the flat. We lay there and I slept in your arms, like in my dreams.

When we woke I realized I had to go to work.

'Of course you must,' you said. 'And I'll walk around and get a feel of the city. Maybe, if I'm brave, I'll call your parents. I don't know if I can put together enough words in Spanish, but I'll try.'

You walked me to the paper and kissed me; I went in as proud as a schoolboy on his first date. From the office I called my Father.

'Here? When? How? Why didn't she ring?' Father was so unexpectedly excited.

I tried to explain you had acted on a whim but it wasn't easy. They wanted to see you that very day. I said you were a little tired and would call them. They didn't ask where you were going to sleep.

Time, to coin a phrase, flew. That night I excused myself early: by midnight I was at the flat. I let myself in. For a moment I was terrified. What if you were not there? But then I saw you, asleep on the mattress. I lifted the sheet: you lay there, naked. I thought I had never seen anything so beautiful. Did you hear me? Maybe, because you smiled. I got undressed very quickly and slid down beside you. I touched you, very gently, with the tips of my fingers, down your back, down your thighs, as Donne has it:

> Licence my roving hands, and let them go,
> Before, behind, between, above, below.
> O my America! my new-found-land. . . .

The shooting stopped for a moment. Now it has started again.

Tuesday, 8 June 1982

You had phoned my mother and gone to see her. She was calm and even lucid. She loved you. 'So elegant! Such hands! She doesn't seem English, does she . . .?' Mother was quite ecstatic. Father arrived as you were about to leave and you had to stay on and have a sherry ('English people *always* drink sherry . . .'). And then it was dinner time and, poor thing, you had to stay for that too, Mother being so worried because there was only roast chicken ('Do English people eat roast chicken? Do they put jam or things like that on it?'). At last you were free: it was almost eleven o'clock.

Then came a welcome surprise from José, one morning as we were enjoying a *maté* at his flat. 'Listen kids,' he said. 'You know my place in Pinamar? Well, it's empty. You could get the paper to let you have your holidays now, couldn't you Enrique? So why don't you take the lady and show her what a sea really is? I don't think they have room in England for beaches like ours.'

But it took me almost two months to get my holidays.

Everyone was away and the paper couldn't spare me. So we had Buenos Aires to ourselves for the time, and finally, in February, we set off to Pinamar by bus. You looked out of the window: I watched your perfect profile against the passing telegraph poles and wondered how so much happiness was possible. You watched the pampas spread out for ever towards the horizon. 'It makes you feel like the centre of the world,' you said, 'turning around yourself, the whole of space and eternity spinning around you.'

José's cottage was tiny, solid, square and clean. It faced the sea: from the windows in the front you could feel the spray and the panes were caked with salt like the porthole of a ship. There was a chimney, and logs for the fire. We unpacked, boiled some water, opened a tin of sardines, and sat with our mugs of coffee by the newly-made fire, munching sardine sandwiches. The house was dark, outside the sea slapped rhythmically against the shore, inside the flames crackled and burst. 'Look at the ghosts in the fire,' I said. 'As a little boy I always saw them. But of course I never told anyone.'

'I think it was Liszt who saw the devil in the fire as a child. When he told his grandfather, the old man slapped his face. "So that you never forget it," he said. And Liszt never did.'

'Maybe we can live in Buenos Aires for a while,' I said. 'Maybe you could study colonial architecture, or something. And then, with a little money, we could go to Europe. Paris if you like. I think I could get a job as a foreign correspondent for the paper.'

We sat there looking at the flames and then made love, and listened to the sea and the wind, till the crying of the gulls woke us up. Sun was streaming in and the day was hot. March, the papers said, was going to be a furnace.

For six weeks we lay on the beach and watched the waves and you told me about Brighton, where you used to go with your parents, and the crazy pavilion built by a prince who had bad taste. The gulls, you said, were the same. 'On other beaches, on other seas, these same gulls have watched us before when we were others.'

'Do you ever think of who you might have been in another life?' you asked.

'Not really.'

'I do. I sometimes feel as if there are certain things I know. I feel that I know something about a fire, and woods, and hunters. In my dreams, sometimes, I see things.'

'That's your Scottish blood. The Scots always see things from the past and the future. The doors are never locked for them.'

'Maybe we've met before, and been together somewhere else. Your hand seems to recognize the feel of my skin.'

We ran into the water: the sand was so white and the water warm and transparent. We jumped when waves came, like children. We dried in the sun and walked. Back at the cottage we felt ravenous. You made an enormous salad and I buttered bread, rubbing it with garlic. 'We'll stink to high heaven,' you said.

Then you smiled. 'I've got a present for you.' You rummaged in your bag and pulled out a small box. 'Smoke,' you said.

I told you I thought you were crazy. 'The nicest thing the men at customs would have done to you is feed you to the tarantulas.'

We ate, and drank, and then we smoked. I turned on the radio. An Argentine crooner was wailing away about his love for the North. We giggled, laughed, roared out loud. I ran over your neck and your breasts with the tip of my tongue. You giggled and then moaned, and held me against you.

Faintly, as if you were here with me, and yet I was next door with the radio, I heard you whisper and the radio speak. You were saying things to me in my ear; the radio had just interrupted its programmes and was announcing something. I strained to hear. A military march, then the news. Argentine troops had invaded the Malvinas to protect a group of junk collectors who had gone over to claim a wreck. You began to undress me, and the voices of the radio drifted away, far away.

Afterwards I wondered if these things happen like this always. My mother remembers how the radio announced the first invasion of the Vietnam War; Granny used to say that the First World War began with someone telling her that in a place she had never heard of a prince of some sort had been shot.

The Malvinas taken. It seemed so funny it made us roll with laughter. You accused me of being a highway robber; I began to shout: 'Down with the imperialists.' We ran out again, onto the sand, the sky was still fiercely blue, the gulls kept on screaming, and then we saw we were still naked. I pulled you to me, we fell, rolled in the sand, hair, hands, in the sand, sand on your lips, tasting of grit and salt, and we made love while the tide moved in, and the waves crept over us, as we came with the waves on the beach.

Wednesday, 9 June 1982

They say this will be our last move. We are about thirty miles from Port Stanley. Samuel has been badly wounded. His arm was cut open by flying ammunition and got infected. He has a fever. The trenches stink; we have the same smell as the sea-lions. Jorge has gone off with a detachment. His parting words were: 'Keep the place clean, my dear. I'll be back in the morning with the bacon.'

You and I locked up José's cottage in Pinamar and went back to Buenos Aires.

The city was full of the Argentine blue and white flag; cars and buses were decorated with banners; military marches replaced European music on the radio and TV. You called the British Embassy: Britain had broken off diplomatic relations and you were told, however, 'not to worry'. 'But try not to provoke anyone,' said the voice on the phone, 'try not to speak English on the street.'

There was a strange euphoria in the city: never had I seen anything like it. People seemed united by mischief, like a nursery rhyme come true. 'The Malvinas *are* now Argentine,' said a little old lady to us as we walked down to my parents' flat. And she waved her little flag at us.

Mother looked very tired: the shouts and the noise seemed to depress her. Father said Mrs Gorritti, the neighbour upstairs, had knocked on the door, asking if she could come in. Her flag had fallen from her balcony onto ours. 'No,' said my mother. 'I'm not dressed.'

'That doesn't matter, Mrs Molina. I'll just pick up my flag. We must celebrate! We've recovered the Malvinas!'

'*You* haven't recovered anything, and you're certainly not going to recover your flag,' said my mother, and slammed the door in the poor woman's face.

On 8 April Alexander Haig arrived in Buenos Aires and my paper sent me to see him. Dozens of foreign journalists were there, flocking around the Sheraton Hotel where a kind of journalists' headquarters had been set up. Haig said that the States were and always had been a friend of Argentina, and that America, North and South, were one. On 30 April the States announced that she was backing Great Britain.

Then, three days later, the *Belgrano*, which the Argentines called a hospital ship, was sunk. The television announced hundreds of dead. The Ministry of Defence was crowded with anxious parents. We sat in my flat and looked out on the city (which you said was like Paris built in London) and counted the lights.

'I never answered you, Enrique, when you said that we would go back to Europe and live in Paris. I think I knew it wasn't right. You rush along. . . . I know you try not to but you do. You are the bulldozer José wrote to me about. I just wanted each day, slowly, to hold and taste. I like each day to be a surprise, and make it, you know, as it happens. You see, I can't believe in what isn't there. I can't say: "I'll do this because then that will happen".'

The next day I received my telegram. Father brought it over. He tried to talk to me, opened his mouth, but then said nothing. I went alone to the recruiting centre. A long line of volunteers stood outside together with the recruits. An old man said he had come to offer his services to the country. 'I'll go and make *maté* for the boys,' he said. 'Down with the bloody *ingleses*!' A sergeant took my name and told me to report the next day at an office in the Ministry of Defence.

We met once more at José's cafe. On the menu, someone had crossed out the words '*budín inglés*' (fruit cake) and written in '*budín Malvinas*'. The Torre de los Ingleses, the English Tower, an ugly reproduction of Big Ben, was re-christened Tower of the Air Force. The Franco-Inglesa chemist on Florida Street took down the second half of its sign and became the Franco. A man reading the *Buenos Aires Herald*, a pro-Argentine publication in English, was beaten up by three thugs.

Over the table at the café I said it was best if you left. There were no planes flying to England any more; you would have to go via Montevideo or Rio.

'I don't want to go,' you said.

'You must.'

Then we sat there, and after a while walked home. My appointment at the Ministry of Defence was at seven next morning. I kissed you but you didn't wake up. I left you sleeping, your hand over your eyes, your hair all over the pillow like spilt wine. I phoned my parents from a public phone and three hours later I was on a plane bound for Bahía Blanca, a training post in the South.

Training post! As soon as we arrived, we were made to line up and a short, dark sergeant arrived to read to us from the Military code. Article after article, page after page, he reeled off the legal jargon. At last he stopped, shut the book with a bang, and lifting his hand to the sky he asked us if we had ever noticed that it bore the colours of our flag. 'That is a symbol, a sign,' he said. 'The sky is our flag, and it will go with us wherever we go. It will blow with the wind of our victory and remind us until the day we die that we are the inheritors of our fatherland. The Malvinas, like the sky, are ours.' And with that he shouted as loud as he could: '*Viva la patria!*' We all began to cheer, but the sergeant lifted his hand once more.

'Cheering will lead us nowhere. It is courage and sweat and heart that we are after. Even cowards can cheer, and traitors can lift their voices. But a true man is only tested on the field.' And he proceeded to list the punishments for each and every kind of disobedience. It began with suspended leave, and carried on through solitary confinement and forced labour to death by firing squad for desertion.

We were tired and hungry and cold, but the speech continued. Now the sergeant began to tell us about the islands themselves. Even though he tried to make the Malvinas sound glorious, the picture he painted was bleak and uninviting. Slowly the questions crept into our minds: Why were we going there? Why did we want to protect these islands? Why did we want these barren rocks lost somewhere in the middle of the sea?

Night fell quickly. Finally, in the dark, we were ordered into our tents: long makeshift lodgings through which the wind whistled steadily. We fell asleep almost before our heads touched the pillows.

The next five days were 'training'. With pieces of wood to simulate guns we were made to aim at painted bull's eyes: the sergeant yelling orders, pretending we had hit or missed, instructing us to aim higher or lower. Many laughed, others followed the rules of the game quite seriously. On the third day we were shown a machine-gun. Another sergeant opened it up in front of us, like a butcher carving his meat and, pulling out the entrails, quickly named the different parts. He then put it together again and departed. Before we reached the battlefield we never actually touched a real gun. On 9 May we landed on the Falklands.

Thursday, 10 June 1982

Now we're leaving the trenches. Grimy, mud still crusted on the uniforms – but who cares. The rain has started again, and the shooting, which had died out for a few hours, has begun, worse than before. They say the English are now barely ten miles from Port Stanley. We are going to march towards them.

Maybe now I just want to stop thinking, end it all, sleep without dreaming. If I am killed here, if my dust will mix with that of the sea-beasts and the Englishmen who died on these rocks before me, I will be an outsider for ever. This land is not my own; this is not my earth, my sky, my sea. All this is as unknown to me as words in a foreign tongue, which I cannot understand, and never will. Once, it seems so long ago now, but it was just a year ago, I told you how much I loved *Dover Beach*, by Matthew Arnold.

> Ah, love, let us be true
> to one another! for the world, which seems
> To lie before us like a land of dreams,
> So various, so beautiful, so new,
> Hath really neither joy, nor love, nor light,
> Nor certitude, nor peace, nor help for pain;
> And we are here as on a darkling plain
> Swept with confused alarms of struggle and flight,
> Where ignorant armies clash by night.

I didn't know then that the poem was ours.

Enrique Molina died in an ambush ten miles west of Port Stanley on Friday, 11 June 1982.